A NEW RIVAL

Amber had finished her warm-up. Now it was time for her to skate with Christopher Kane, the star of the ice show.

Jill glanced over at Ludmila, a top coach at the International Ice Academy in Denver. Ludmila was watching Amber intently. Jill saw Ludmila smile as Amber completed a series of perfect camel spins.

"They really look good together," Jill forced herself to say.

"Well, Ludmila seems to think so," Tori remarked. "I wonder if she'll ask Amber to the Academy someday."

Jill stared at Tori. Someday? What about now? Jill's stomach dropped. What if Ludmila asked Amber to the Academy instead of Jill?

NUTCRACKER ON ICE

Melissa Lowell

Created by Parachute Press

A SKYLARK BOOK
NEW YORK · TORONTO · LONDON · SYDNEY · AUCKLAND

With special thanks to Darlene Parent, director of Sky Rink Skating School, New York City.

RL 5.2, 009–012

NUTCRACKER ON ICE

A Skylark Book / December 1995

Skylark Books is a registered trademark of Bantam Books, a division of Bantam Doubleday Dell Publishing Group, Inc. Registered in U.S. Patent and Trademark Office and elsewhere.

Series design: Barbara Berger

ISBN 0-553-48353-6

Published simultaneously in the United States and Canada

Bantam Books are published by Bantam Books, a division of Bantam Doubleday Dell Publishing Group, Inc. Its trademark, consisting of the words "Bantam Books" and the portrayal of a rooster, is Registered in U.S. Patent and Trademark Office and in other countries. Marca Registrada. Bantam Books, 1540 Broadway, New York, New York 10036.

PRINTED IN THE UNITED STATES OF AMERICA

OPM   0 9 8 7 6 5 4 3 2

1

"The scouts are ready now," Kathy Bart announced.

The members of the Silver Blades skating club gathered around their coach. They had just finished trying out for a very important show. Four scouts were at Silver Blades to find skaters for parts in the *Nutcracker on Ice* spectacular. The scouts had already visited other skating clubs all over the country. The Silver Blades club in Seneca Hills, Pennsylvania, was their last stop.

Nutcracker on Ice was going to be taped in Boston and then shown on national TV. And the stars of the show were none other than Christopher Kane and Trisha McCoy—two of the world's most famous figure skaters!

Jill Wong felt her heart pound with excitement. More than anything, she wanted to skate the part of Clara.

After all, the story of *The Nutcracker* was all about Clara: about the nutcracker toy she was given for Christmas, and how the nutcracker was really an enchanted prince who took Clara on a trip to the Land of Sweets. Jill knew she could be a terrific Clara. Plus she had another very special reason for wanting the part.

Everyone knew that Jill was one of the best skaters in Silver Blades. The year before, she had been chosen to train at the prestigious International Ice Academy in Denver, Colorado. It was a great honor. And a lot of hard work. But to Jill, working hard at the Academy was a dream come true. And she would still have been in Denver, working hard, except for her accident.

It had happened when Jill was home on spring vacation. She had gone hiking with her new boyfriend, Ryan McKensey. Ryan was two years older than Jill. Jill was fourteen now, but had been only thirteen when she met Ryan. She had been a little nervous around him and his friends. So Jill had started showing off when they'd all gone hiking, leaping from rock to rock on the trail. But her antics had proven disastrous when she took a bad fall and broke her left foot.

What had happened next was tough for Jill. She had had to tell Ludmila Petrova, a coach and one of the owners of the Academy, that her foot was broken and she couldn't come back to the Academy. Worst of all was the fact that no one had known when—or if—Jill would ever skate again.

But Jill did skate again. After months of physical therapy, she was skating better than ever now. One part of her was happy to be back home again. It felt comfortable to be back at Silver Blades, skating in the familiar rink at Seneca Hills. And it was definitely fun to be back at school with her old friends. But another part of Jill couldn't wait to return to the Academy. Skating was the most important thing in Jill's life. And returning to the Academy was a major step in her skating career.

Jill was definitely ready to return. But she had to convince Ludmila. Then auditions for *Nutcracker on Ice* had been announced. This was it, Jill knew. This was her chance! If she could win the role of Clara, everyone at the Academy would see her perform on TV. Ludmila would definitely want Jill back in Denver.

"Listen up, everyone!" Kathy Bart beamed at the skaters gathered around her. "Your auditions were terrific," she told them. "I'm so proud of all of you!"

A murmur of relief went through the crowd. Kathy was a top coach, and she was tough. The Silver Blades skaters had nicknamed her Sarge. Kathy hardly ever gave them praise like this. It made them all feel really good.

Kathy paused and took a deep breath. "But here's the biggest news," she continued. "The talent scouts agree—they've found the perfect skater for Clara, right here in Silver Blades!"

Haley Arthur and Nikki Simon screamed out loud. Jill yelled and hugged her two friends. Jill's long black braid bounced as they all leaped up and down.

"I knew it!" Haley squeezed Jill tightly. "I just knew

Silver Blades was the best! I wonder who they chose. Oh, Jill—maybe it's you!"

"I hope so," Nikki agreed, grabbing Jill's hand. "You really deserve the part, Jill."

Jill grinned. Both Haley and Nikki were pairs skaters. Haley's partner was Patrick McGuire. Patrick and Haley both had bright red hair and dark brown eyes. When the two of them were on the ice, they made a really striking couple. Jill thought they'd skated great and would definitely get a role in the ice show.

Nikki skated with Alex Beekman. Nikki had a delicate look. Her wispy brown bangs set off her bright green eyes and a sprinkling of freckles across her nose. Nikki was on the thin side. Her partner, Alex, had broad shoulders and dark curly hair. Alex was one of the cutest male skaters around, and a terrific pairs partner. Nikki and Alex looked fantastic on the ice. For a while Nikki had been worried that Alex wanted to be her boyfriend—and Nikki already had a boyfriend! But it had all been a misunderstanding. Now Nikki and Alex were the best of friends, on and off the ice. Jill hoped their audition would land them a role in the ice show, too.

"Thanks, guys, for thinking I have a chance at skating Clara." Jill smiled at Haley and Nikki. "I hope the scouts agree with you."

Since neither Haley nor Nikki was competing for the role of Clara, Jill knew they really meant it when they wished her the best of luck.

Jill crossed her fingers behind her back. Please let Clara be me! she said to herself.

Kathy caught Jill's eye and smiled at her. Jill felt her hopes soar. She knew her audition performance had been good. And Kathy seemed to think so, too. Now Jill only hoped the scouts felt the same way!

Jill joined Haley, Nikki, and another skating friend, Martina Nemo, as they crowded around the three scouts. "Who is it?" everyone asked at once. "Who's going to be Clara?"

Please let it be me, Jill wished again silently. Please— I've just *got* to be Clara!

Someone pushed Jill from behind. She turned and found herself staring into Amber Armstrong's hazel eyes. Jill's stomach did a sudden flip-flop. Amber! Jill had almost forgotten about her.

Amber was eleven. She and her mother had recently come to Seneca Hills to check out Silver Blades. The club was one of the best in the country, and visitors were often stopping by. Many skaters hoped to join the club and train there, but only a few were accepted. As soon as Jill had seen Amber, though, she had known there was something different about *this* visitor.

For one thing, the younger girl had a smooth, effortless skating style. She already had many advanced jumps in her program, and she made the difficult moves look easy. But there was something else about Amber—something Jill didn't like. Wherever Jill went, whatever Jill did, Amber was there, watching her! And asking a million nosy questions. It was driving Jill crazy.

She'll be gone soon, Jill had kept telling herself. Amber was only visiting. In a few days, Jill had thought, she and her mother would go back to New Mexico, where they lived. Then everything would be back to normal. Only it hadn't happened that way.

Somehow Amber had learned the entire Clara audition routine. And she had skated it for the scouts. In fact, Amber had skated it so well that she'd become a member of Silver Blades—right on the spot! Now there were two favorites for the role of Clara: Jill and Amber. One of them would be Clara. But which one?

Amber caught Jill's gaze, but Jill quickly turned her eyes away. As she did, Jill felt Haley poke her in the ribs. Haley gave Jill a thumbs-up sign. "Don't worry," Haley whispered. "Amber's good, but you're better."

Jill squeezed Haley's arm. "Thanks," she whispered back.

"Quiet, everyone," Kathy called. "Dan has an announcement."

All heads turned toward Dan Trapp. The blond coach was also a new member of Silver Blades. He had come to fill in while their other coach, Franz Weiler, was in the hospital. Mr. Weiler had been with Silver Blades for many years. But he had recently had a heart attack, and no one was sure when he would return. In the meantime, Mr. Weiler's students needed a coach. That coach turned out to be Dan Trapp.

Dan was a surprise to everyone. His style was so different from Mr. Weiler's. Mr. Weiler was strict, and because he was older, he sometimes acted like a father to his skaters. Dan was young and acted more like a big brother. Plus Dan liked to work on a skater "from the inside out." Sometimes he asked a skater to *think* through his or her program, instead of skating it!

Jill liked Dan's new ideas. But not everyone agreed with her.

Dan rocked back on his heels and beamed at everyone around him. "Kathy's right," he announced. "You all skated your best—and that's what counts. Only a handful of you will win parts in this ice show. But your work as skaters goes on no matter what! So you *all* deserve a big round of applause."

Dan began to clap loudly, and soon everyone joined in. Jill clapped the loudest of all. Haley gave Jill another big smile. Nikki and Martina also wished Jill good luck.

"And now," Kathy began, "I think the scouts should announce who has the role of—"

Suddenly there was a commotion near the door of the rink. A raspy voice rang out. It got louder and louder. Jill gasped. She knew that voice. It belonged to Tori Carsen's mother.

Jill exchanged a look of surprise with her friends.

"Stop! Stop! There's been a terrible mistake!" Mrs. Carsen hurried toward the scouts, pushing her way through the crowd of skaters. Behind her, Jill saw Tori's blond curls bobbing as Tori raced to catch up to her mother.

Tori Carsen was a good friend of Jill's. She was also

one of Silver Blades' most promising skaters. Or she *had* been. Just the day before, Tori had quit Silver Blades. Tori was one of the skaters who *didn't* like Dan Trapp. She and Dan had had a huge fight, and Tori had stormed out of the rink. Everyone had been amazed that Tori would actually quit—right before the big audition.

"Wait! Wait for me!" Tori wailed. She rushed over to the boards, where Kathy and Dan were standing.

"Kathy!" Mrs. Carsen practically screamed. "Just a minute, *please*! Tori's *got* to audition. She didn't quit! It was all a terrible mistake. You *must* give her a second chance."

Mrs. Carsen nudged Tori with her elbow, pushing her right under Dan's nose. "Tori has something she wants to say. Go on, Tori," Mrs. Carsen whispered.

Tori blushed a little. She glanced at Dan before looking down at the floor. "I'm sorry about yesterday," she mumbled. "I really didn't mean what I said." Then she looked up eagerly. "I *do* want to audition for *Nutcracker on Ice*!"

"Oh, no!" Jill gasped out loud. Instantly she turned red with embarrassment. Haley, Nikki, and Martina stared at her. But Jill couldn't help it. If Tori was allowed to skate, it could change everything. Tori could get the role of Clara instead of Jill or Amber!

Jill caught Amber's eye. The younger girl had a look of astonishment and worry on her face. Jill could see that Amber didn't want Tori to audition, either.

But I *do* hope Tori gets to skate, Jill decided right

then. Tori is a good skater. She deserves a chance, too. She's my friend, Jill thought. And after all, fair is fair.

Kathy stared at Tori and then frowned at Dan. Dan walked over to the scouts. "What do you say?" he asked them. "Do you have time for one more audition?"

2

The tall scout with dark hair pointed at his watch. He started arguing with the blond woman scout who stood beside him. Dan put a hand on the tall man's shoulder. "Tori's a super-duper skater," Jill heard Dan say. "It's your loss if you don't give her a go."

Meanwhile Tori rushed to a nearby bench. She pulled her skates out of her rose-colored skate bag and quickly began to lace up. Tori was already wearing her skating outfit—a gray velvet skating dress trimmed with black at the collar and cuffs. She looked great, as usual.

Tori's mother could be really pushy, but she was also a terrific clothing designer. She made all of Tori's skating outfits herself—and they were always beautiful. Mrs. Carsen had once skated competitively herself. She had never had great success. But now she'd decided that Tori could be the famous skater in the Carsen family. Mrs. Carsen really encouraged Tori to skate her best every day—and to look her best every day, too.

"I can't believe Tori's back," Nikki whispered to Jill and Haley. "She really doesn't like working with Dan."

"I guess Mrs. Carsen changed Tori's mind," Haley answered, grinning. Haley and Tori were best friends. No one knew better than Haley how much Mrs. Carsen pushed her daughter. "I'm glad, though," Haley added. "No offense, Jill—your audition was great. But Tori deserves a chance to try out for Clara, too."

"You're right," Jill agreed.

At the side of the rink, Dan clapped his hands. "All right!" he cried out loud. He rushed over to where Tori sat on the bench. "You are one lucky girl," he said. "The scouts will let you audition. But they're not too happy that you're late. So don't spend a lot of time warming up. Just do your best, Tori. Be the champ I know you are."

"No problem," Tori said seriously. "I'm going to be great."

Jill watched Tori glide smoothly onto the ice. Her friend's blue eyes were full of confidence. Tori quickly warmed up, stretching her hamstrings before doing a couple of waltz jumps, a spin, and a single axel. Next she practiced the double Lutz–double loop combination—and landed it perfectly. Tori grinned. She raised a hand and signaled to Mr. Ortega in the sound booth that she was ready. Tori struck her opening pose, and the music began.

The first jump in the Clara routine was a triple toe loop. Jill watched as Tori prepared for the difficult move. She began on her left forward inside edge, with her left arm and shoulder in front of her and her right arm and shoulder held to the back. Then Tori extended her free foot and prepared to step onto her takeoff foot.

Jill thought Tori looked great—and eager to do everything right. Maybe a little *too* eager. Jill narrowed her eyes. Tori bent far forward at the waist as she reached to place her left toe pick in the ice behind her. Jill knew what that meant. She drew in a deep breath. Sure enough, Tori completed her three rotations, but as she finished the jump her upper body was way ahead of her landing foot. Her foot wobbled badly, and she reached one hand down to steady herself.

There was a murmur of surprise from the crowd. Tori looked shaken. Then she recovered and continued the routine.

"I can't believe it," Jill whispered, turning to Haley. "Tori bent way too far forward on her takeoff!"

Haley nodded. "She was trying too hard. Oh, well." She looked at Jill. "It's between you and Amber now."

Jill felt a flutter in the bottom of her stomach. "I guess so." She turned to see what the scouts thought of Tori's performance. As she did she caught Amber watching *her* instead of Tori. Jill felt a stab of irritation. Why did Amber always watch her every move, on the ice and off? Either Amber couldn't stop competing for even a minute, or else the younger girl was just obnoxious. Whichever it was, it really made Jill angry. She turned away from Amber and concentrated on Tori again.

Tori swept into the next part of the program with strength and precision. She was smiling, and looked relaxed and natural. As the music soared, Tori lifted into a double axel and then went into a flying camel. After that she powered around the rink, gathering speed for the double Lutz–double loop combination. She landed it perfectly and closed with an elegant layback spin.

Jill burst into applause. It took real guts to skate so well after making a mistake right at the beginning of the routine.

Jill rushed to the boards with Haley and Nikki to congratulate Tori as she came off the ice. Martina joined them. So did Danielle Panati. Danielle used to be a member of Silver Blades. But she had decided she was more interested in being a writer than a skater. Nowadays she was a reporter for the school newspaper. Jill knew Danielle was there to cover the auditions for the paper.

"Tori, that was great!" Haley gave her best friend a giant hug. "I'm so glad you came back today."

"Silver Blades wouldn't be the same without you," Jill agreed. And I really mean that, too, she thought.

Tori bit her lip. "Thanks, I guess." She looked totally disappointed. "I really blew that triple toe loop. I'll never get the part of Clara now."

Jill patted Tori's arm. She felt a little awkward. It wasn't always easy being friends with the same people you had to compete against. Still, Tori *was* a close friend. Jill shook herself and forced a bright smile. "Hey—you did *great,*" she told Tori. "Maybe you won't be Clara, but you deserve a part in the show."

"Jill's right," Danielle agreed. "And talk about making a dramatic entrance! This will be a great item for my story." She whipped a reporter's notebook from the pocket of her blue jeans. "What made you change your mind about coming to the auditions?" she asked Tori.

"Well, I talked with my mom this morning," Tori said. "You can guess how mad she was. She couldn't believe I stormed out of here yesterday." Tori glanced at Danielle's notebook. "But don't put that part in your story," she said.

"I won't," Danielle promised. "I don't want to embarrass you. In fact, what I'm really interested in is what it's like to switch to a new coach right before an important audition."

Tori rolled her eyes. "It's awful, that's what it's like," she said. "Especially when the new coach is so weird."

Tori began to describe what working with Dan was like. She told Danielle how Dan liked everyone to get in a huge circle and hold hands, then lean back as far as possible. The point of the exercise was to trust your teammates. They were the ones who kept you from falling.

Many of the Silver Blades skaters, including Jill, thought the exercise was terrific. In fact, Jill thought Dan's ideas about teamwork made everyone feel better about the club and about themselves. But Tori thought

Dan's exercises were a bore. She also felt that the way he liked skaters to think through their routines was a giant waste of time.

"And my mother agrees," Tori told Danielle.

"Really?" Danielle said, opening her eyes wide. "But she still wanted you to audition?"

"She did," Tori admitted. "And I'm glad we finally talked it over. Because I realized that even though I may not like Dan's coaching, that isn't a very good reason to give up these auditions. I've worked too hard." Tori grinned. "Besides, we're talking about *national TV*!"

"Hey, look," Haley suddenly shouted, "the scouts are leaving! I wonder what's going on."

Everyone turned to see the four scouts leave the ice rink. Dan and Kathy had serious expressions on their faces.

"I hope my audition didn't make them leave," Tori said. She looked nervous. "I know I bobbled that landing, but the rest of the routine was pretty good. Wasn't it?"

"Tori, you did really well," Jill said. "It can't have anything to do with you."

Haley nudged Jill. "Kathy and Dan are heading this way. Now we'll find out what's going on."

Nikki sighed. "At last! The suspense is killing me."

Jill watched as the coaches approached the skaters. Her stomach felt as if it were doing somersaults. She couldn't remember feeling this nervous about anything since she'd broken her foot and didn't know if she'd ever skate again.

All around her, kids were chatting. It was pretty loud.

"All right, everybody," Kathy said. "Settle down. The scouts had to rush off to catch a plane. But Dan and I know their decisions."

Tori breathed a deep sigh of relief. Haley let out a nervous giggle. Danielle stepped closer to Jill and put a hand on her arm.

Kathy gave the whole group a stern look. "Listen up, now," she told them. "I know you're all anxious, so let's get right to it—again."

Jill crossed her fingers and squeezed her eyes shut tight. Please let Clara be me, she thought. Please!

3

Kathy took a deep breath. "Five of you got parts in the ice show," she announced with a smile. "You'll get valuable experience. And terrific exposure. Not everyone your age gets to appear on TV with stars like Christopher Kane and Trisha McCoy."

Kathy paused. Jill's stomach was still doing flipflops.

"I'll announce pairs first," Kathy said. "Haley Arthur and Patrick McGuire, you'll be skating the part of Mother Ginger's children in act two."

Patrick hugged Haley and spun her around wildly. Nikki and her partner, Alex, were standing right next to them. Jill could see them and the other pairs skaters trying not to show how disappointed they were. A murmur ran through the crowd as the skaters reacted.

"Quiet, everyone! You'll have plenty of time to talk

later." Kathy raised her eyebrows. "Tori, even though you came running in late, you've won a part, too."

Tori gasped. "Which one? Who am I?"

"You're one of the mice in act one," Kathy answered.

"A *mouse*?" Tori looked astonished. "That's all?"

"That's great news, Tori," Dan told her.

"I came back here to be a mouse?" Tori looked less than thrilled. "I don't believe it. This can't be—"

"Now, as for Clara . . . ," Kathy went on, interrupting her.

Jill sucked in her breath. This was it. This was what she had been waiting for! Danielle reached out and squeezed Jill's hand tightly. "It's you, Jill," Danielle whispered. "It has to be!"

Jill thought so, too. She couldn't help it. She felt a smile spreading over her entire face.

Kathy cleared her throat. For a moment Jill thought there was an awkward look in Kathy's eyes. "The scouts have decided to give the role of Clara to our newest member, Amber Armstrong," she said.

Danielle gasped and turned to Jill. The smile faded from Jill's face. Her cheeks burned with embarrassment. She felt as if everyone were staring at her. Amber was going to be Clara!

Jill felt hot tears rush into her eyes. She couldn't even look at Kathy. How had Kathy let this happen? Her own coach had let them give Jill's part away—to an eleven-year-old! Then Jill felt a sudden pang of fear. Maybe Kathy didn't think Jill was a good skater anymore. Maybe Kathy wanted to spend more time coaching Amber.

Jill felt sick as she thought about it. After all, Amber was younger than Jill. Maybe Kathy thought Jill's career was already finished. Maybe she thought Jill hadn't made a good recovery from her broken foot. Maybe Kathy thought that Amber would be a champion by the time she was Jill's age.

Jill swallowed hard. She had to get away. With her head down, she turned to push her way through the crowd.

"Jill," Kathy said sharply, "don't leave yet!" There was scattered laughter from the group of skaters. Jill stopped. She felt her cheeks flame an even brighter red as everyone looked at her.

"I have one more announcement," Kathy said. "Jill, the scouts decided to give you the role of the Dewdrop Fairy." Kathy smiled right at her.

Somehow Jill managed to nod quickly at her coach. Then she stared down at the floor. The Dewdrop Fairy? That role wasn't even listed on the poster announcing the auditions. It had to be a really small part. Jill knew from having read *The Nutcracker* that there was a Dewdrop Fairy who appeared in the Land of Sweets. But what kind of skating part would it be?

Whatever it was, it wasn't Clara. Clara was the lead. The whole story of *The Nutcracker* was about her. Jill wanted to be Clara. She needed to be Clara!

"Congratulations to you all," Kathy was saying.

"Super job, everybody," Dan added.

The crowd began to scatter as the skaters broke into small groups and walked away. Jill saw more than a few disappointed faces. Meanwhile, Jill's friends rushed up to her. She swallowed hard and tried to pretend that everything was fine. There was no point in letting everyone see how upset she was. Especially not Amber.

"Jill, we're going to Boston together! Aren't you excited?" Haley hugged Jill. "This is so great! Where did Patrick go?" Haley raced off to find her partner.

"Congratulations, Jill. You must be really happy," Martina said quietly.

"Yeah," Jill answered. She tried to smile. After all, Martina had worked hard, but she hadn't gotten a part. She didn't have the advanced moves, such as the triple toe loop, that Jill and Amber already had.

"I'm sorry you won't be in the show, Martina," Jill told her.

Martina shrugged. "Well, I had hoped to get a smaller role. Maybe one of the mice." She paused. "And now Tori, one of the best skaters here, is going to be a mouse. I guess these auditions were tougher than anyone thought."

"Yeah, including me," Jill admitted. "No one did as well as I expected." Except for one person, Jill added silently. Amber. Amber had won the lead role—on her first day as a member of Silver Blades!

Tori pushed her way over to Jill, her hands on her hips. "What is the matter with those scouts? Can you believe I'm supposed to be a *mouse*?"

"It's not the worst role," Martina said. "The *Nutcracker* story is all about mice."

Tori made a face. "Oh, please!" Then she caught Jill's eye. "You must be furious, Jill. If *I* couldn't be Clara, at least it should have been you! Not Amber. She has no experience at all! This is an important show. What if she messes up on camera? It makes no sense."

Just then Dan walked over to the group. Amber was with him. "I'm so proud of all my skaters," Dan said. He beamed at Jill, Tori, and Amber. "Just think, you'll soon be skating with Kane and McCoy!"

Amber's cheeks were pink with excitement, and there was a big smile on her face. "This is so great," she crowed to Jill. "We both made it into the show! And I've only been in Silver Blades for about twenty minutes!" Amber was practically jumping up and down.

Jill didn't know what to say. "Yeah, it's great," she mumbled.

Danielle pulled Jill aside. "Are you okay?" Danielle asked in a low voice.

Jill bit her lip. Danielle was a good friend. But Jill didn't trust herself to tell Danielle her true feelings right then. She was afraid she might cry.

"It's too bad about Clara," Danielle added softly.

Jill gazed at her friend gratefully. So Danielle *did* know how she felt after all.

"I just can't believe Kathy let this happen," Jill replied. "She's been my coach for so long. Maybe she likes Amber better than me."

"Oh, Jill. She couldn't!" Danielle looked shocked.

"And that's not all," Jill said miserably. "I had it all

worked out. Skating Clara was going to be my way to get Ludmila's attention. I thought she'd see me on TV and invite me back to the Academy."

"Well, she'll still see you on TV," Danielle reminded her. "And Ludmila will be impressed no matter what part you skate."

Jill shrugged. Danielle was just trying to make her feel better. And it wasn't working very well.

Dan clapped his hands. "All right, now, *Nutcracker* skaters. Amber, Tori, Haley, Patrick, Jill—we're having a meeting in Kathy's office," he announced. "So let's head on over there."

Dan had called her name last, Jill noticed. Was she already the least important one there?

The others hurried into the office. Tori grabbed Jill's arm, and the two of them followed more slowly. "This really stinks," Tori complained to Jill. "I wanted to skate with the stars, not in some stupid rat costume! And on top of that, I'll have to listen to Dan the whole time. All his speeches about positive thinking . . ." Tori shuddered.

"At least your coach likes you," Jill said quietly. She felt a lump rise in her throat. "Kathy's so impressed with Amber, I'm not sure she thinks much of my skating anymore."

"Really?" Tori stared at Jill. "Boy, you must really hate Amber. I don't like her much, either," she added. "Remember when Mr. Weiler got sick? I thought Kathy would coach me for a while. Then Amber came along, and Kathy decided to coach *her* instead. That's why I got stuck with Dan."

"You're right," Jill said. "I guess Amber's messed things up for both of us."

"And she's such a phony," Tori continued. "The way she came up to you just now. Like she was *so* happy that you got in the show, too." Tori shook her head in disgust.

By the time Jill and Tori reached the office, the meeting had already started. Kathy gave them a stern look as they found seats.

"Now we have a different kind of announcement," Kathy said. "Something special. The producers of the show had a great idea. They've decided to interview some of the skaters. You know, to do a behind-the-scenes segment as part of the TV show. But they need to tape right away. So they're sending a camera crew to your practice sessions here at Silver Blades, and—"

"You're kidding!" Tori interrupted. "I'm going to be interviewed? That's great!"

"Cool," Haley cried. "We'll all be TV stars!"

Patrick looked really pleased. "Hey, I'll get everyone some of my dad's T-shirts to wear. It'll be great publicity for his business."

"Hold on a moment," Dan said. "Let Kathy finish."

"As I said, they'll do interviews with *some* of the skaters." Kathy hesitated. "The truth is, they chose two of you—Amber and Jill."

Tori gasped. Haley and Patrick looked upset, too.

"I'm sorry," Kathy apologized. "It was the scouts' decision. If it were up to me, I'd have them interview all of you."

Amber didn't seem to notice how upset the others were. "They're going to interview *me*? Really?" Her hazel eyes were shining.

"What exactly will they do?" Jill asked.

"They'll tape you at practice and at home," Kathy said.

"At home?" Suddenly Amber looked concerned.

Kathy nodded. "They want to show a typical day in the life of a promising young skater."

"Then why interview only Jill and Amber?" Tori asked, sounding hurt. "We're *all* promising young skaters."

"True enough, Tori, true enough," said Dan.

Jill barely heard the others talking. An interview on national TV! Now everyone who watched the ice show would get to know Jill as an up-and-coming skater. No wonder Tori was jealous. In competitions, all the skaters tried to get the audience cheering for them. Some skaters thought that when the audience was rooting for a skater, it even swayed the judges into giving them better marks. This interview could be an opportunity to make tons of new fans.

But Jill was also a little nervous. The Wong family was so big, and the younger Wongs were definitely a handful! Jill wasn't sure they would make the right kind of impression on television. What if the twins started fighting, or her sister Randi started playing the violin? What if her father went on and on about what a cute, chubby little baby Jill had been? What if her mother started giving out her favorite Chinese recipes? It could be totally embarrassing. If only the TV crew didn't have to come to her *house.*

Then Jill thought of something even worse. What if Amber looked better than Jill on TV? Amber had those enormous hazel eyes and that big, wide smile.

But when Jill glanced over at Amber, she was surprised to see that Amber was staring down at her hands in her lap. In fact, Amber didn't seem at all excited anymore. She even seemed a little worried.

Jill felt a flare of anger. What does *she* have to worry about? Jill thought. She has the leading role!

". . . for tomorrow's taping," Kathy was saying.

Jill bolted up straight in her chair. "Tomorrow? The TV crew is coming tomorrow?"

There was no time to worry about Amber now. Jill had more important work to do. Someone had to get the Wong family ready to be on television!

4

"**R**andi Wong!" Jill yelled at her seven-year-old sister. "I just cleaned this whole room. What are you doing?"

Randi looked up from the coffee table. "Coloring," she said.

"You can't color in the living room!" Jill scooped up the pile of crayons and paper and dumped it in Randi's lap. "The TV crew is due any minute!"

Jill sighed. It seemed as if every time she turned around, one of her brothers or sisters had made another mess. And everything had to be perfect for her big interview. Jill pointed at the crayons and paper. "Take those to your room," she ordered. Randi made a face as she left.

Jill's mother smiled at Jill as she entered. "Don't

worry, sweetheart. It's going to be fine." Mrs. Wong put an arm around Jill's shoulders. "Relax!"

"I can't help it, Mom. I've cleaned this room four times already."

Mrs. Wong laughed. "Tell me about it! With seven kids around, I'm always cleaning up after somebody. But the TV crew—"

Mrs. Wong didn't get to finish. Just then Jill's eleven-year-old brother, Henry, ran into the room. He threw himself onto the floor and peered under the couch. A second later he bounced up and began searching under the couch cushions. There was a worried look on his face.

"Henry!" Jill straightened the cushions. "Be careful. What are you looking for, anyway?"

"Spidey! I can't find him anywhere!" Henry cried. He poked behind the living room curtains.

Jill turned pale. "Spidey! Why would he be in here?"

"Because he's not in his spider cage," Henry answered.

"Oh, no!" Jill wailed. "The TV people are coming and you let your pet *tarantula* get out?" Spidey was huge and hairy. He looked dangerous, but he wasn't. He wouldn't hurt any of the TV crew. But he sure could scare them.

Jill groaned. "I can't believe it! Why does this have to happen now?"

"Jill, calm down," Mrs. Wong urged. "Getting hysterical won't help anyone. Henry, did you check your room carefully?"

"I looked everywhere," Henry said. "I just fed him his cricket. And when I turned around, he was gone."

"Henry," Mrs. Wong said seriously, "you're not just playing a trick on your sister, are you?" She peered at him over her glasses.

"No, Mom." Henry grinned. "But thanks for the tip. I'll remember that for another time."

"Henry!" Jill wailed again. She turned angrily to her mother. "Mom, *do* something!"

"Henry," Mrs. Wong ordered, "go check your room again. I'll take the kitchen. Jill, look in here some more." Her mother patted Jill on the cheek as she hurried into the kitchen.

Randi raced back into the living room with another of Jill's sisters, Kristi, who was nine. They were both wearing scuba masks on their faces and had long scarves draped over their shoulders. Randi carried a butterfly net. They hurried over to the coffee table and began knocking a pile of magazines onto the floor.

"Stop! What are you two doing?" Jill screamed.

The girls stared at her in surprise.

"We're on an expedition," Kristi announced.

"We're helping Henry find Spidey." Randi giggled.

"I'll find Spidey. You go upstairs and take that stuff off," Jill commanded. As Jill straightened the pile of magazines the telephone rang.

"Jill! Phone call!" her mother shouted.

Jill ran into the kitchen to pick up the phone. "Hello?" she said.

"Jill! Hi! It's me, Bronya!" said the voice on the other end of the line.

"Bronya!" Bronya Comaneau had been Jill's roommate at the International Ice Academy. Jill hadn't heard from her in weeks. Bronya was from Romania. She was a year older than Jill, and very serious and quiet.

"How are you?" Jill asked.

"I'm great, and you must be, too," Bronya said. "I heard you were picked for *Nutcracker on Ice*. Me too! We can see each other in Boston."

"That's fantastic, Bronya. I'm so happy!" Jill answered. "What part did you get?"

"Not a big one. I skate with some other kids in the party scene in act one."

Jill knew the party scene well. It was mostly a group of boys and girls playing games around the Christmas tree. None of their roles was very big. Jill was surprised, because Bronya and the others from the Academy were some of the top skaters in the country. If they only got to skate in the party scene, Jill's role as a fairy must be *really* small.

"What's your part?" Bronya asked.

"Oh, I don't know much about it yet," Jill said. "We just had our auditions yesterday. The scouts came to Silver Blades last."

"Well, I'm sure it's a great role," Bronya said. "And I can't wait to see you again. It will be like old times. And guess what? Ludmila is coming, too."

"She is?" Jill was surprised. Ludmila always had a

million things to do at the Academy. The famous Russian coach had trained many Olympic champions back in the 1980s, and she was very demanding. But that was why Ludmila was also one of the most important people in the world of ice skating. Jill had never expected that Ludmila would travel to Boston for the ice show.

"It might be good if Ludmila saw you skate in Boston," Bronya said. "Maybe then she would ask you back to the Academy."

Jill chuckled. "I thought that, too," she admitted.

"Maybe it will come true then," Bronya said. "I have to go now, Jill. You know how it is here. Practice, practice, practice." She laughed. "See you in Boston! Bye, Jill!"

"Bye, Bronya. Thanks for calling." Jill stared at the phone and chewed her lip. Suddenly she felt really nervous. Even Bronya had known that this show could be Jill's chance to impress Ludmila. Jill just had to go back to the Academy. But how could she impress Ludmila as a silly fairy?

"Waaah!" Jill's mother rushed into the kitchen with two-year-old Laurie in her arms. Laurie was shrieking at the top of her lungs. "Jill," her mom said, "did you find Henry's spider?"

"What?" Jill felt distracted. "Uh, no. I forgot. Bronya called, and—"

"Well, then," her mother interrupted, "will you take Laurie upstairs for her nap now?"

"Sure," Jill answered. "And I'll try to find Spidey, too." Jill started up the stairs. She bounced the baby on her hip, but Laurie didn't stop crying. Then the phone rang again. It kept ringing. Jill realized that no one was going to answer it.

Do I have to do *everything*? Jill wondered as she grabbed the phone in the upstairs hall.

"Jill, hi, it's Haley!"

"Hi, Haley." Laurie screamed even more loudly. Jill bounced her faster.

"Wow, what's that awful sound? Sounds like a fire-truck siren," Haley joked.

Jill was in no mood to laugh. "I can't talk now, Haley!" she snapped. "Laurie's screaming. Henry's pet spider is missing. I don't even know where my father and the twins are. And the TV people are coming any minute!"

"Sounds normal to me," Haley said. "My parents are always screaming these days. They'd probably have a fight right on national TV."

Jill was suddenly sorry she'd snapped. It wasn't the first time that Haley had mentioned her parents' fighting lately. "They're still not getting along?" she asked with concern. But before Haley could answer, the doorbell rang downstairs. "Oh, Haley, sorry, that's the doorbell! It must be the TV crew!"

"No problem. We'll talk later. Good luck!" Haley hung up.

Jill slammed down the phone. With Laurie still in

her arms, she ran downstairs. She pulled open the front door with a big smile on her face. But there was no television crew standing outside.

Jill's mouth dropped open. "Tori! What are you doing here?"

5

Jill stared at Tori in surprise. Laurie stopped crying and gazed up at their visitor.

"You invited me over to see your Christmas tree, remember?" Tori said, smiling. "So I thought I'd come by." She craned her neck to peek behind Jill. She put her hand on the door to open it wider.

Jill noted that Tori looked awfully dressed up for a casual visit. She wore an emerald-green sweater and a green-and-black plaid skirt with matching black tights and loafers.

"Tori, I'm sorry." Jill held the door only half open. "This really isn't a good time. The TV crew is coming to interview me. Did you forget?"

Tori pushed right past Jill and stepped into the hallway. "No, I didn't forget. In fact, I had a great idea. They want to film a typical day in the life of a young skater, right? So, what's more typical than one of your friends stopping by? A friend who also happens to be in the ice show?"

Jill sighed. "No one said anything about friends being in my interview," she told Tori. "Besides, I'm crazy right now. Everything here is a wreck."

"Great!" Tori said with a big smile. "I can help out. Now, what's the trouble?"

Jill gave up. "Oh, okay." She shifted Laurie in her arms. "First you can help find Henry's lost tarantula."

"What?" Tori shrieked, throwing her arms up in the air. "You mean there's a deadly spider loose in here?"

At the sound of Tori yelling, Laurie began to cry again. Through the open front door, Jill saw a van pull up outside. The camera crew!

"Here!" Jill shoved Laurie into Tori's arms. "Take her. I've got to find that spider."

Jill raced into the living room. Her father was on the floor with the five-year-old twins, Michael and Mark. He was helping them build a fortress of blocks.

"Dad!" Jill cried. "What are you doing? Spidey is missing, the room is a mess—and the TV crew is here!"

Mr. Wong laughed. "Calm down, Jill. This is the real us. I don't think they'll mind a few blocks on the floor."

Jill groaned. "What if Spidey runs across my lap or something in the middle of the interview?" she wailed.

"He won't. Spidey is right here, see?" Mr. Wong pointed inside the fortress on the floor.

"There's a dragon in our dungeon!" Michael whooped.

"Yeah, he's a big bad monster," Mark chimed in.

Jill turned to the twins. "At least be good for the TV people, okay?" she told them. "No fighting or calling each other names. And no spilling grape juice on the carpet, or—"

There was a knock at the door. Mrs. Wong let in a dark-haired man in a black leather jacket and jeans. He was followed by two more men and a woman. They all carried video equipment. As Jill watched them, they began to set up cables and lights around the living room. The man stopped to look curiously at Tori, who was still holding Laurie.

"You don't look like one of the Wong family," he said, puzzled.

"Hi! I'm Tori Carsen." Tori grabbed his hand. "Jill's best friend—I'm also in *Nutcracker on Ice*."

Jill hurried over. "I'm Jill Wong," she said.

The man shook Jill's hand. "I'm Bill Blair. This is my crew. Are you ready for your interview?"

As Jill opened her mouth to answer, the twins knocked over their fort. There was a loud crash.

"Spidey's loose!" Mark and Michael yelled at once.

Jill winced. "Ready as I'll ever be," she answered with a sigh.

"Okay, then. Let's do it." Bill went behind the camera and pointed it at Randi and Kristi. "All right, kids. Who wants to tell me what it's like to have such a talented sister?"

"Kristi's going to be an astronometer," Randi bragged.

"She means an astronomer," Henry corrected. "And it's not so special having a sister who skates. Except when you get to be on TV!"

Bill laughed and pointed the camera at the twins. They both clapped their hands over their mouths. They glanced at each other and then back at Bill.

"Are you guys interested in skating?" Bill asked.

The boys looked at each other and shook their heads, making a face to show how *not* interested in skating they were.

Mrs. Wong frowned at them. "They feel shy in front of the camera."

"Well, don't worry about making any mistakes," Bill reassured everybody. "We can always cut things out. Just be yourselves and pretend the camera isn't here. Randi, do you like to watch Jill skate?" Bill tried again.

Randi nodded. "Yes, but it makes me sad when she goes away to school." Randi smiled sweetly and snuggled up to Jill.

"I miss her, too," said Kristi. "This much!" She spread her arms wide and knocked over the plant on the end table. Dirt spilled onto the rug. Mrs. Wong ran into the kitchen for the vacuum. Laurie started playing in the dirt.

"No, Laurie!" Jill cried.

Randi tried to pull the baby away.

I'll get her!" Henry said, grabbing Laurie.

"No!" Randi yelled. "Let me help!"

"No, me," Kristi said. She began tugging at Laurie, too.

"Uh, maybe now would be a good time to interview you alone, Jill," Bill suggested.

Mr. Wong helped Henry take Laurie upstairs. Randi and Kristi followed them. But the twins stayed on the couch.

"Boys, your turn is over," Bill said. He glanced around and spotted Tori. "Tori, that's your name, right? Can you help us out here?"

"I'm ready!" Tori hurried over to sit on the couch.

"Actually, I was hoping you could take the twins upstairs," Bill told her.

"Oh, sure," Tori said, but she looked disappointed.

With the room clear, Jill felt nervous again. After all, this interview was going to be on television!

Bill peered through the camera. "Jill, you have such a close-knit family. Was it hard to be away from home when you were at the Ice Academy?"

"Definitely. I missed everybody so much. I'm really used to having my brothers and sisters around," Jill answered.

Then she thought of something. What if Ludmila saw the interview and thought that Jill was saying she didn't want to go back to the Academy? "But of course they have great coaching at the Academy," Jill added quickly. "Way better than what I can get here," she blurted.

Tori had just returned to the living room. She gave a little gasp. Jill saw a funny expression on her friend's face.

Oh, no! Jill realized that she had just insulted Kathy Bart's coaching!

"No, no, I don't mean that," Jill said. "I mean Kathy, my coach here, is the best." She stopped. Wouldn't saying that insult *Ludmila*? "Well, uh, maybe not the best," Jill stammered. "I mean, not the only best."

"Well, there can be only one best, right, Jill?" Bill grinned.

"Right. I mean, no!" Jill flushed and looked down at her hands. Now she was all mixed up! "What I'm trying to say is, Kathy's a great coach for me here. And Ludmila is a great coach at the Academy. They're both great."

"Well, where would you rather be?" Bill asked. "Here at Silver Blades, or back at the Academy?"

Jill gulped. Now what should she say? "Well, uh—" she began.

"Eek!" Tori suddenly screamed.

"Spidey!" Jill saw something dark and hairy scurry across the living room rug. "I'm sorry," Jill cried. "But I've got to catch a tarantula!"

Bill shrugged. "Okay. We'll call it a wrap."

Jill couldn't believe it. Her first big interview, and she had managed to insult both her coaches! She had never felt worse.

6

"Just a few more hours," Kathy called over her shoulder to Jill. "We'll be there by lunchtime!"

The Silver Blades skaters were finally on their way to Boston to tape the ice show. The ride seemed to take forever.

Jill glanced at Kathy and recalled the TV interview she had done for the ice show two weeks before. She had told Kathy the interview hadn't gone well. But Kathy didn't know Jill had insulted her. Jill hoped that part would be edited out.

To get her mind off the interview, Jill thought about her busy schedule. She and the rest of the skaters would be in Boston for four days. Two days would be spent rehearsing their scenes. The third day they would have a morning practice and a dress rehearsal in the afternoon. On the morning of the fourth day they would tape the show. Afterward they would drive home in order to reach Seneca Hills in time to celebrate Christmas Eve.

The past two weeks had sped by as they all learned their new parts.

Jill had worked hard to learn the Dewdrop Fairy role. She'd been surprised to find that it was a much longer routine than she had expected. It was harder, too, with several challenging moves. The most difficult was a triple flip–double loop combination. Jill frowned, thinking about it. She'd had trouble landing the flip and moving into the double loop. She was a little worried about doing it well in Boston. And worried that she wouldn't perform the routine well enough to impress Ludmila.

Jill snuggled into her seat as the van sped down the highway. The van was really comfortable, with dark blue plush seats and big sight-seeing windows. Outside there was a light dusting of snow on the trees.

Tori glanced out the window. "It really looks like Christmas now," she remarked to Jill, who was sitting beside her.

Jill nodded. "I know. It was pretty hard leaving my family with Christmas only five days away!"

Haley turned around in the seat in front of Jill's, where she was sitting next to Patrick. She winked. "And don't forget, Jill—you have something special to look forward to."

Tori spoke in a singsong voice. "Ryan is coming to Boston!"

"You are so lucky!" Haley said. "I can't believe Ryan has cousins in Boston, and that his parents are letting him drive up to stay with them. You must be so excited that he can come watch you tape the show!"

Amber leaned across the aisle. She was sitting next to her mom, who had fallen asleep as the van left Seneca Hills.

"Hi, Mouse! Hi, Dewdrop!" Amber giggled. "My mom's been calling me Clara all week," she explained. "Dan says it helps you get into the part."

"That's nice," Jill mumbled.

Amber grinned at Jill. "You're so lucky you have a boyfriend," Amber said. "He's really handsome. I bet he's really nice, too, huh, Dewdrop?"

Tori nudged Jill in the ribs. Jill frowned. "Amber," she said to the younger girl, "this is a private conversation. And please call us by our regular names."

"Oh," said Amber, looking disappointed. "Okay."

Tori nudged Jill again. "Good for you," she whispered.

Jill giggled. "No way am I going to call her Clara all week."

"Hey, did you guys see this article in *Skating Magazine*?" Haley held up a copy of the magazine for everyone to see. "It's all about Trisha McCoy and Christopher Kane!"

"I already read that," Tori answered. "It said they're having tons of fights lately. I can't believe they're really in love when they're always arguing."

Haley shrugged, trying to look casual. "I don't know. My parents fight a lot, but that doesn't mean they don't love each other."

Jill and Tori exchanged a look. "Uh, that's true," Jill said, trying to make Haley feel better. All of Haley's friends knew that her parents weren't getting along.

"Lots of couples fight," Jill continued. "But they make up. Like me and Ryan."

Not too long before, things had gotten mixed up between Jill and Ryan. It had happened right after the *Nutcracker* auditions were announced. Ryan had been acting very mysterious, and Jill had thought he didn't like her anymore. She had imagined that he wanted a new girlfriend—one who didn't spend so much time skating. Jill didn't know that Ryan had made special plans for them. He had arranged a romantic sleigh ride for the night before Christmas Eve. He had been awfully disappointed to find out that Jill might be in Boston that night.

Jill and Ryan had talked and realized that nothing was wrong between them. And instead of a sleigh ride, Ryan had given Jill a special gift. It was a lovely bracelet of linked golden hearts. Jill wore it all the time.

"Did you and Ryan have a big fight?" Amber asked.

Jill rolled her eyes. Did Amber always have to know everything about her? Even her private life?

"It's okay, Amber," Tori said. "It was only a misunderstanding. Jill and Ryan are totally okay now."

"If I had a boyfriend, I'd *never* fight with him," Amber said. "I think Kane and McCoy are silly. I think any couple that fights is silly, and—"

Tori was about to say something when Haley cut in. "At least Kane and McCoy don't skate pairs," Haley said. Jill could tell she was trying to change the subject. "I mean, they're just two skaters who happen to be in love. They don't have to practice together all the time, like Patrick and me."

Patrick gave her a playful punch on the shoulder. "Hey, I'm just glad you don't have to be in love to skate well," he teased.

"But I bet it helps." Amber twisted in her seat to stare at Jill. "Right, Dewdrop?"

Jill rolled her eyes. Amber just wouldn't get the hint! "I asked you not to call me that," Jill said.

"Oops. Sorry," Amber said.

"What's this about Kane and McCoy?" Dan asked, turning around to join in the conversation. "Another article about their rocky romance?" He chuckled. "They need to lighten up. We all should! I know—why don't all we sing something to make the time pass? How about a round of 'Row, Row, Row Your Boat'?"

Tori winced. "I don't think so, Dan. We're not in kindergarten anymore."

"Well, neither am I, but I still like singing," Dan said cheerfully.

Somehow, even with Dan singing loudly most of

the time, they got to Boston sooner than Jill expected. Before she knew it, the van was pulling up in front of the Hotel Sinclair, where all the skaters in *Nutcracker on Ice* were staying. Jill looked out the window and saw the big city bustling around her. People bundled up in thick winter coats hurried by. Many carried shopping bags stuffed with Christmas presents.

As everyone piled out of the van Dan whipped out a camera. "I think we should start a Silver Blades scrapbook," he said. "For all our greatest moments. Smile! It's Silver Blades history!" He snapped a photo.

"Come on, everybody," Kathy called.

Amber climbed out of the van ahead of her mother. "Excuse me, Kathy," Jill heard Amber whisper, "but will this trip cost much? This van is so fancy! And what about the hotel and everything? It must be really expensive."

"Not at all," Kathy said. "I already told your mom. The producers are paying for everything. Being in this show won't cost you any money. So don't worry."

Amber sighed in relief. Jill was startled that Amber was worried about money. She glanced at Amber's mom, who was getting out of the van. Amber was lucky that her mom could travel with her to Boston. Jill's parents didn't have that choice. Her dad often worked overtime to help pay for Jill's skating. And when her mom wasn't working at her part-time job, she was home taking care of the kids.

"Listen up," Kathy called, interrupting Jill's thoughts.

She held up a hand for attention. "Let's unload our things and check into the hotel quickly."

"Great!" Jill said. "Do we get to see the rink right away?"

"We get to *rehearse* right away," Kathy answered. "I know we're all tired from the ride, but the rehearsal schedule's pretty tight."

"Remember," Dan said, "we have only three days to rehearse. We tape on the fourth day. We'll have to keep our energy flowing!"

"When is his energy ever *not* flowing?" Tori said under her breath to Jill.

A doorman in a dark uniform with gold buttons opened the hotel door. The lobby was decorated with red carpets and drapes. A Christmas tree hung with red and gold ornaments stood near the front desk.

Kathy checked them in, and Dan organized the last of the bags and equipment from the van.

"I've got our room assignments," Kathy announced. "We're all on the same floor. Dan will share with Patrick. I'll share with Amber's mom. And you four girls will share two rooms. Amber, why don't you go with Haley?"

"Okay!" Amber smiled at Haley. "I'm so glad I get to share with you instead of my mom. It'll be fun."

Haley nodded. "Yeah, fun," she told Amber.

Tori nudged Jill. "It's kind of strange *not* having my mom with me," she whispered. Usually Mrs. Carsen went to shows and competitions with Tori. But Jill knew that Tori's mother was working hard at home.

Mrs. Carsen was finishing some designs for a new line of clothes.

"I wish *my* mom were here, too," Jill agreed. "I'd love to have her see me skate my first TV role."

Tori tossed her head. "Well, I bet if I were skating Clara, my mom would've come along—even if she had to bring her work with her!"

Kathy and Dan had gotten the room keys. They handed them out, and everyone headed to the elevator.

"Do they have room service?" Patrick asked. "I'm starved."

"They have lunch for us at the rink," Kathy answered. "Unpack your things, and we'll go over there in the shuttle bus. Bring your practice clothes and skates with you." Kathy paused. "Dan and I are responsible for all of you. So no wandering off without telling one of us exactly where you're going. Agreed?"

Everyone nodded. The elevator came, and they went upstairs to find their rooms. Jill and Tori unlocked and opened their door and set their bags down. Inside the room were two beds, two dressers, and a TV. A huge basket of fruit, wrapped in pink cellophane, sat on a table.

"Ooh, look!" Tori exclaimed, picking up the note attached to it. " 'Happy holidays and best wishes to our skaters, from the producers of *Nutcracker on Ice*.' " She grabbed an apple and started to eat it. "I feel just like a professional."

"Me too," Jill agreed.

"You should," Tori said. "I mean, you're being pro-filed in that special interview."

"Oh, yeah," said Jill. "That." She wanted to put the disastrous interview out of her mind. She opened her suitcase and began to hang her clothes in the closet. Tori hoisted her three matching red suitcases onto the bed. Then she began to unpack also.

"Hey, did you hear?" said Tori. "Dan told me they're going to tape the show in front of a live audience. You know, to make it more like a regular show in an arena."

"That's great," Jill said. "Maybe I can get Ryan a pass." She picked up the telephone receiver. "I'll make a quick call now and tell him about it. He's supposed to drive up tomorrow. I'll just check that his plans haven't changed."

Jill reached Ryan and confirmed that he would arrive the next afternoon. As Jill hung up the phone after their happy good-bye, she noticed that Tori's side of the closet was already stuffed with outfits.

"Tori, did you bring your entire wardrobe with you?" Jill asked with a laugh.

Tori shrugged. "You know we Carsens like to dress up."

"Well, don't take too long," Jill said. "Kathy and Dan are waiting."

They finished quickly and were soon in the shuttle bus. Minutes later, they arrived at the Boston Skate Club rink. Patrick and Haley went with Dan to grab a bite of lunch. Jill, Tori, and Amber were scheduled to begin their practice in a few minutes. Kathy told them they would have to eat afterward.

Jill stared around the rink. She was amazed by all the TV equipment set up there. There were lights and cables everywhere. Cameras on wheels were positioned all around the rink. And two huge cameras were hanging on cranes over the ice.

"Do you think McCoy and Kane are here yet?" Jill asked.

Amber shrugged.

"All I see are kids," Tori answered.

Tori was right. A dozen or so skaters were rehearsing in the middle of the rink. There were a few adults, but most were junior skaters. They seemed to be acting out the beginning of *The Nutcracker*, in which the guests arrive for Clara's family's big Christmas party.

"There's Bronya!" Jill waved wildly at her friend. Across the ice, Bronya caught Jill's eye and waved back. Jill spotted Marie LaFontaine, another skater from the Ice Academy.

"Tori, you've got to meet Bronya and Marie, two of my friends from the Academy," Jill said, pointing them out.

Amber moved closer to Jill. "Wow!" she said in excitement. "I can't believe all these cameras. And all the people! This is amazing, isn't it, Dewdrop?"

Jill didn't answer, so Amber turned to Tori. "Isn't this amazing, Mouse?" Amber asked.

"What's amazing," Tori answered, "is that you forgot to call me by my real name."

"Oops. Sorry," Amber said.

Tori glanced at Jill. But Jill was searching the rink. If Bronya and Marie were there, Ludmila must be around, too. As Jill scanned the rink she noticed two interesting-looking women, both fashionably dressed in bright-colored leggings and loose sweaters.

One woman was blond, with a very short haircut. The other woman had pulled her brown hair back from her face in a tight bun. They were sitting on the bleachers watching the skaters closely. The woman with the bun leaned forward and pointed at a skater who had just completed a smooth flip jump. The blond woman nodded and wrote something in her notebook.

"I wonder who they are," Jill murmured.

Tori glanced at the bleachers. "Maybe choreographers or something," she said.

Kathy hurried over. "Amber, get ready! They need you to rehearse Clara with the party guests. Hurry and change so you'll have time to warm up. Jill and Tori, you too. You're not needed right away, but you can warm up now."

"Okay, sure, Kathy," said Jill.

Kathy walked away. Amber glanced at Jill. "Come on, Dew—I mean Jill. Aren't you going to change like Kathy said?"

"In a minute," Jill answered. Tori nodded in agreement.

"Okay, see you." Amber left with a little wave.

Jill was still scanning the crowd for Ludmila. The rehearsal on the ice ended, and Bronya hurried over.

"Jill, I'm so happy to see you," Bronya said in her Romanian accent. She and Jill hugged each other.

Tori gave Jill a little poke in the ribs and cleared her throat. She nodded toward Bronya.

"Oh, Bronya, this is my friend Tori Carsen," Jill said. "Tori, this is Bronya Comaneau."

"Oh, Tori, Jill told me all about you!" Bronya cried.

"She told me about you, too," Tori said. "I can't believe I finally get to meet you!"

"You look great, Jill," Bronya said in admiration. "Breaking your foot has been maybe good for you?"

"Definitely not good," Jill said with a laugh. "But you look great, too. You cut your hair, right?"

"Yes. I was tired of my long hair. Do you like my new look?" Bronya cupped her hand under her chin-length bob. The new haircut set off her eyes and made her long neck look more graceful than ever.

"It looks super," Jill replied. She lowered her voice a little. "Is Ludmila here? I haven't seen her yet."

"Oh, yes," Bronya answered. "She's here somewhere." The Romanian girl looked around the rink. "She'll appear when you least expect it, if I know her. And I *do*!"

Jill felt a little nervous. She wasn't sure what she should say when she finally saw Ludmila.

Bronya nodded toward the rink. Jill spotted Amber warming up on the ice.

"She is terrific," said Bronya, watching Amber with admiration. "Is this the girl from your club who will be Clara?"

"It sure is," said Tori, frowning.

"She's in the next party scene," Bronya said. "Clara is on the ice for almost the whole time."

"I guess she gets to skate with Trisha McCoy and Christopher Kane," Tori said enviously. "Have you seen them yet? I mean, shouldn't they be here by now?"

"I haven't seen them, but they should be here soon. Everyone's dying to meet them," Bronya answered.

"I can't wait," Tori gushed. "I think I get to skate with Christopher Kane, too. I'm in the first act."

"What role?" Bronya asked.

Tori hesitated. "I'm a mouse," she admitted, flushing red.

"Oh, the mice have such good routines!" Bronya cried. "And I'm sure they get to skate with Christopher Kane." She turned to Jill. "What scene are you in?"

"I'm not sure," Jill answered. "But it's in the second act. After Clara and the Nutcracker Prince go to the Land of Sweets."

"Oh! That's when Trisha McCoy has her big Sugar-plum Fairy solo," Bronya said. She frowned. "But you won't get to skate with McCoy or Kane, then."

"I won't?" Jill felt her stomach fall in disappointment.

"Haven't you seen the script?" Bronya looked surprised. "It lists the characters in each scene," she explained. "In the second act, Christopher Kane mostly skates with Clara."

Jill felt herself flush. In the *Nutcracker* ballet she had seen, the prince danced with the Dewdrop Fairy. Jill had just assumed that meant she'd skate some part of her routine with Christopher Kane. It had never occurred to her that the ice show would be different.

Bronya saw that Jill was upset. "I'm sorry," she said. "But Clara *is* the most important role."

"Oh, I know that," Jill said in a low voice.

"Listen," Bronya told them, "I've got to get something to eat. Nice meeting you, Tori. See you later, Jill?" She gave her friend another hug.

"Sure, Bronya. See you later," Jill replied. Then she forced herself to smile. "I guess we'd better get changed," she said to Tori. "We're supposed to be warming up."

Jill picked up her skate bag and headed toward the dressing room. She stood up straight and concentrated on walking with her head held high.

It doesn't matter that I don't have the best part, she told herself. A professional always does the best she can. And I'm going to skate my best, she vowed. No matter what!

7

Jill changed quickly. As she walked toward the ice she reviewed the Dewdrop Fairy routine in her mind. Over and over again she pictured each move in her program. Suddenly she bumped right into someone.

"Oh, sorry, I—" Jill began.

"Why, Jill! Hello!"

Jill looked up to find a small woman with very short brown hair standing in front of her.

"Ludmila!" Jill gulped. She couldn't believe she had bumped right into her former coach. "Oh, Ludmila, excuse me!"

"It's nice to see you again, Jill," Ludmila said seriously. Jill glanced at Ludmila's long nose, strong chin, and straight, dark eyebrows. The coach seemed as stern as ever.

Jill knew that Kathy had called the Academy once or

twice to give Ludmila a progress report. Kathy had told Jill that Ludmila was pleased to hear she was recovering well from her broken foot. But Ludmila had never asked to speak to Jill. And Jill had been afraid to call Ludmila and speak to her directly.

"Uh, it's nice to see you again, too," Jill finally said. "Really nice." She felt her face turn red.

"Congratulations on your role." Ludmila gave Jill a smile of approval.

"Thanks," Jill replied awkwardly. Does Ludmila think the Dewdrop Fairy is the best role I could get? She worried. Or is Ludmila just trying to be nice? Of course, if I'd been picked to be Clara, she really *would* be impressed.

"Well, at least I'm skating really well," Jill blurted out.

Ludmila gave her a funny look. "It is an honor to be in this show," the coach told her. "I look forward to seeing your performance."

"Thank you." Jill paused. Was that it? Wasn't Ludmila going to say anything more? Or was she waiting for Jill to speak next?

"Oh, Jill," said Ludmila, "I meant to ask you something."

This was it! Ludmila was going to ask her if she wanted to return to the Academy! Jill crossed her fingers behind her back.

"Yes?" Jill asked eagerly.

"How is Franz Weiler?" Ludmila asked. "I heard he had a heart attack. How is he doing?"

"Oh. I think he's much better," Jill answered, trying not to let her disappointment show. "But no one knows when he'll be back at the rink."

"I'm sorry to hear that," said Ludmila. "If you speak to him, please give him my best. I'll see you later, Jill."

Jill's heart sank as she watched Ludmila leave. She was convinced that she hadn't said any of the right things. Ludmila had acted happy to see her, but Jill knew that no matter what Ludmila said, the real honor was to skate the role of Clara. Plus Ludmila hadn't said anything about Jill's going back to the Academy.

Jill made her way to the ice. The two women she had noticed earlier were still seated in the bleachers. They watched Jill, and one began to write in her notebook. Jill shrugged. She was too upset about Ludmila to think about anything else.

She slipped off her skate guards and glided over to a corner of the huge rink. Kathy was already there, waiting. The ice was crowded with people. Members of the television crew were everywhere. Some of them were setting up different camera angles, while others were rehearsing the set changes. Jill was still amazed by how many people it took to produce a television show.

Kathy told Jill to warm up and to relax her muscles. Then they would run through the entire routine.

"Ready?" Kathy asked after about ten minutes.

"Definitely," Jill answered.

Jill raised her arms across her chest in her start position. Practicing her routine would take her mind off all her worries. When she skated, nothing else ever seemed important. She took a deep breath and began.

The Dewdrop Fairy's routine started with a few steps on the points of her skates, almost like a ballerina. Jill executed them with precision. Then she glided backward into a couple of easy waltz jumps before stepping into a back camel. She arched her back and reached backward until she could grab hold of her left skate. She had to complete four rotations in that position. The move was hard for her, but she was improving.

"Good," Kathy encouraged her from the side. "Keep going."

Jill released her skate and finished the spin. Then she stepped into a series of backward crossovers, which looped in a figure eight. A straight line step sequence was the setup for the difficult triple flip that came next. She glanced away for a split second just before her setup and noticed that the two women on the bleachers were still watching her intently. Jill held her breath as she dug her toe pick into the ice for the takeoff.

Jill wobbled as she landed the triple flip, and she had to use all her strength to complete the two rotations of the double loop. Okay, Jill, she told herself, focus!

She twirled into a dizzying change-foot sit spin. By this time she was more than halfway through the routine. Her mind was racing. She hadn't flubbed the triple flip–double loop combo, so she was skating almost perfectly. She began to feel really good about how she was doing.

Jill smiled happily and launched into another set of

crossovers before jumping into a triple salchow–double toe loop combination. As her body lifted into the air she felt strong and in control. She did her final spin, reaching over into an elegant layback. She came to a dramatic finish, punching her toe into the ice to skid to a complete stop. Then she crossed her arms in front of her chest again, with her hands fanned out like a frame around her face. She closed her eyes and smiled.

"Not bad," Kathy called. "It's starting to look first-rate."

Starting to? Jill repeated to herself. Kathy was always hard to please, but Jill had worked hard on this routine. Except for her trouble with the triple flip, she thought the program was already strong.

"I'll work harder," Jill said.

"Good! Then let's try it straight through one more time," Kathy told her.

Jill took some deep breaths. She shook out her arms and legs as she prepared to go through her routine again. The two women on the bleachers were still watching her. They were nodding and talking enthusiastically. But before Jill could ask Kathy who they were, Bill Blair came toward her. His shoes made him slip and slide across the ice. He was with some of the TV crew who had taped Jill's interview in Seneca Hills.

"Hey, Jill," Bill greeted her. "That looked great! Could you do some of your routine again? We'd like to tape it for your behind-the-scenes segment."

Jill glanced at Kathy. "Is it okay?"

"Why not?" Her coach nodded. "But Jill," Kathy

warned, "keep your mind on your work—not on the camera."

As Jill went back to her start position, she noticed Amber rehearsing on her own nearby. Amber had a lot of choreography to learn, since she was in so many scenes. Jill shook her head. This was no time to think about Amber. She had to concentrate on her own routine.

Jill glanced at Bill Blair behind his camera. Then she began to skate again, preparing for the waltz jumps. She turned into the back camel with good momentum. But when she arched her back and reached for her left skate, she lost her balance and fell with a thud.

She got right up again, shaking her head and brushing the snow off her black leggings. Kathy gave a little nod as Jill continued with the rest of her routine. Jill couldn't help noticing that Amber was staring at her. So what? Jill told herself. Everyone falls in practice. Even Amber.

Jill continued smoothly, without making any big mistakes. She was surprised at how tired she felt, though. It really was a demanding routine.

Jill glided over to the side of the rink to catch her breath. Kathy nodded in approval. "Not bad," her coach said. "You should be ready in time."

Bill hurried over with another camera operator. "How about answering a few more interview questions for us, Jill?"

Jill hesitated. She didn't want to make any more mistakes, especially not with Kathy watching.

"I'll go easy on you," Bill promised.

"Okay, then," Jill said.

"It must be very hard to keep working on those jumps and spins after you fall. How do you do it over and over again?" asked Bill.

Jill laughed. "Well, you can't improve if you won't let yourself fall again and again," she said. "It's probably one of the hardest things to learn. But if you want to be a top figure skater, you always have to keep trying. Eventually you get it right."

"I bet you get really tired at the end of a long day," Bill commented.

"Absolutely. Once I even fell asleep at the dinner table. My mom had to wake me up so I could go to bed," Jill explained.

She noticed the cameraman glancing to one side. Jill followed his gaze and saw that Amber was right behind her. Just at that moment Amber lifted into a big double Lutz–double loop combination. Even Bill Blair stopped asking questions to watch.

Jill gaped in astonishment. Amber had performed the jump combination right where the camera was pointed. Jill was certain Amber had done it on purpose.

She turned back to Bill and searched her mind for something to say that would get his attention again. But before she opened her mouth, Bill signaled the camera operator to stop taping.

"That's all for now, Jill," Bill told her. "You get some rest. I'll be talking with you soon."

Kathy thanked Bill. Then she turned to Jill. "I need

to speak to Amber. Why don't you grab some lunch now?"

Jill watched as Kathy and Amber skated to the other side of the rink. "Bill, wait," Jill called out quickly. She hurried after the interviewer. "Can I ask you something?"

"*You* want to do the asking now, huh?" He chuckled. "Sure. What do you want to know?"

"Well, um, you said something when you first interviewed me," Jill began. "That if there are parts of the interview you don't like, you can always cut them out." Jill wanted to ask him to cut out the stupid things she had said about her two coaches.

"Oh, right," said Bill. He smiled. "Don't worry. We won't be cutting much from *your* interview. You'll have plenty of time on-screen. I'd better go, Jill. My crew's waiting. Thanks again!"

Jill sighed in frustration as Bill hurried away. He had misunderstood her completely. Now she'd never get the chance to change her interview. She racked her brain, trying to remember whom she had insulted more—Kathy or Ludmila.

Shaking her head, Jill stepped off the ice. She slipped on her skate guards.

"Excuse me."

Jill glanced up. The two women she had noticed earlier stood in front of her.

"We want to congratulate you on your fine skating," the woman with the bun said. She had a thick French accent. "Allow me to introduce myself. My name is Monique Descartes. And this is my colleague, Jeanne Bonet. We are from the International Ice School of Paris."

"The Paris Ice School!" Jill cried. "I've heard all about it!" The school was very famous. Jill knew that many Olympic skaters had trained there. "Wow. It's really nice to meet you," she said as politely as she could.

"It's lucky for us to meet you," Monique replied. "You see, we are here because some of our skaters are in Boston to perform in an exhibition. Jeanne and I have a lot of free time. When we heard they were taping this ice show, we came right away. So exciting!"

"And we are very impressed with your skating," Jeanne added. "In fact, we were wondering if you knew about our training center. We happen to have a spot open for a truly exceptional skater."

"You mean you want to talk to me about going to your school?" Jill gaped at her in surprise. "In Paris?"

"Yes. Paris is a lovely city," Monique said. "And our school has beautiful facilities—four Olympic-sized rinks and the latest in weight-training equipment." She shrugged. "Who knows? Perhaps you might consider training there one day."

Jill hesitated. "I don't know," she said. "I never thought about training in Paris. I mean, Europe is so far away."

"Of course," Monique agreed. "It is something to think carefully about. You will need to talk with your parents. Are they here?"

"Uh, n-no," Jill stuttered. "Just my coach. My parents never travel with me."

"I see." Monique seemed impressed. "Then you are already very independent. Maybe Europe is not so far away for someone like you. Would you mind if I send a brochure about the school to your hotel room? You could read more about it. See what you think. Perhaps we will talk again."

"Well, sure. Why not?" Jill said, feeling flustered. She gave Monique her name and room number. They said good-bye.

Jill's head was spinning. The two women were definitely impressed by her skating. It felt great. Things are looking up, Jill thought.

She still wanted Ludmila to ask her back to the Academy, but just in case the coach didn't, it would be good to have another choice. What would another school be like? Jill wondered. How would it feel to be asked to train at the International Ice School—in Paris?

8

At eight o'clock the next morning Jill glided to her start position on the ice. It was hard to believe that this was already their second full day of practice. The next day would be their third in Boston. They would practice in the morning and have their dress rehearsal after lunch. And then they would tape the show the next day.

The earliest rink time that day was reserved for junior skaters with solo roles. The other skaters practiced off the ice while they waited their turns. Jill noticed that Haley and Patrick were busy nearby. And Ludmila was across the rink, working with her skaters from the Academy. Jill wondered if Ludmila would speak to her again before morning practice ended. So far Ludmila hadn't even glanced Jill's way.

Jill had already finished working with Kathy. So had Tori. Now Kathy was coaching Amber.

"Excellent work, Amber," Jill heard Kathy shout. "Excellent!"

"It felt good," Amber replied cheerily.

Jill tried not to feel bad. She knew it was babyish to be jealous of Amber. But it hurt that Kathy seemed so pleased with the younger skater. It seemed as though Sarge had never given Jill that many compliments.

Jill was just about to begin her routine when the doors of the rink flew open. Angry, loud voices filled the arena. Jill ignored the noise and struck her opening pose again. Then she realized that everyone else had stopped practicing.

Jill and Tori skated over to the side of the rink. "What's going on?" Jill asked a tall blond girl.

"It's Trisha McCoy and Christopher Kane," the skater said in excitement. "They're finally here!"

Everyone was talking and whispering and trying to get near the doors. Jill couldn't wait to see the two stars in person.

As Jill and Tori watched, Trisha McCoy marched in. Her long, wavy red hair was flying behind her. She wore a green sweater and leggings tucked into boots, with a matching green silk scarf floating around her shoulders. She looked incredibly beautiful. She also looked pretty angry.

"Don't you *dare* tell me how to skate!" Trisha yelled, waving her hand at Christopher Kane as though she was trying to get rid of him. Her emerald-green eyes flashed. "I am perfectly capable of performing my own routines!"

Christopher Kane was right beside Trisha, an annoyed expression on his face. Jill thought he looked really cool in faded jeans and a white T-shirt under a black leather jacket. He seemed taller in person than on TV. And he was even better-looking, Jill decided. His closely cropped dark hair really set off his warm brown eyes.

Jill and Tori pushed closer to get a better look.

"Trisha," Christopher said, raising his voice, "*you're* the one who asked for my advice!"

"Well, I didn't ask you to *insult* me!" she shot back.

"I wasn't insulting you!" Christopher cried. "I just mentioned that your arm movements looked stiff. I thought you wanted a flowing line."

"*I'll* decide what I want, thank you!" Trisha said through clenched teeth. "And right now I want you to go away!"

Jill couldn't believe it. There were dozens of people standing around, including a group of young skaters who idolized the two stars. Yet Trisha and Christopher didn't seem to notice anyone.

"Trisha, you're being ridiculous!" Christopher stopped walking and folded his arms. "I'm not chasing you through this rink. If you want to discuss this, you'll have to do it right here!"

Trisha whirled around and glared at him. Everyone was staring. Jill was amazed by the whole scene. Her parents disagreed sometimes, but they never had fights like this. It was like something out of the movies.

"Well, maybe I *don't* want to discuss it," Trisha replied furiously. "Maybe I never want to talk to you again! Why would I want to talk with someone who has absolutely no appreciation for my skating? I don't even want to be seen in the same show with you!" She raised her chin. "I'll be in my dressing room. *If* you decide to apologize." She tossed her scarf back around her neck and rushed away.

One of the producers hurried over and put his arm around Christopher's shoulders. They talked quietly for a few minutes.

"Okay, everybody," the producer called, "let's take a break. We'll get a fresh start after lunch—with Ms. Mc-Coy."

The big fight was all anyone could talk about on the shuttle bus back to the hotel. Kathy and Dan had stayed at the rink for a coaches' meeting, so the skaters were on their own with Mrs. Armstrong.

"I was so embarrassed watching Kane and McCoy fight like that," Amber said to everyone when they were all seated in the hotel café. "Weren't you embarrassed, Jill?"

Jill shrugged. She *had* been embarrassed, but she didn't want Amber thinking she felt the same way as an eleven-year-old. Jill wanted Amber to believe she was much more mature.

"It really sounded awful," Haley said quietly.

"Oh, big stars like that are always temperamental," Tori said. "Nobody cares. I just think it's exciting that they're finally here."

A uniformed waiter came over to the table.

"What would you like, miss?" the waiter asked Amber.

Amber turned to Jill. "What are you having, Jill?"

Jill glanced at Tori and rolled her eyes. Can't Amber decide anything on her own? her look said. But at least she didn't call me Dewdrop, Jill thought.

"I'll have chicken salad and an orange juice," Jill ordered.

"Me too," Amber said right away.

"I'll have that, too," Haley told the waiter. She gave Amber a smile.

"I'll have the turkey club special," Patrick said, "a baked potato, and a chocolate shake, please."

"Wow!" Haley said. "You must really be hungry."

"I am." Patrick grinned. "It takes tons of energy to lift you up in the air all day," he teased. "I need to eat a lot."

Haley frowned. "I don't weigh *that* much," she complained.

"Maybe you don't think so," Patrick said, laughing. "But it's because I'm strong enough to carry you around!"

"What are you saying?" Haley stared at Patrick. Her cheeks turned pale. "Are you trying to start a fight with me?"

"Better watch out, Haley," Tori teased. "Patrick might storm off like Trisha McCoy did!"

Haley suddenly pushed back her chair and stood up.

"I guess I'm not very hungry," she mumbled, rushing away from the table.

"What's wrong with her?" Patrick asked.

Jill frowned. "I'll go after her," she said. She found Haley on a sofa in the lobby. "What's wrong?" Jill asked her quietly.

Haley turned to Jill with a worried look on her face. "I'm sorry, Jill. I know I'm acting silly. But it's all this talk about Kane and McCoy fighting." Haley took a deep breath. "My parents have been fighting nonstop lately." She brushed tears away from her eyes. "I'm afraid that without me there this week, things might fall apart."

"Oh, Haley, don't worry," Jill reassured her. "Everybody fights. Even my parents don't get along sometimes. And Tori's right about Kane and McCoy. Sure, they had a huge fight. But I bet they're back together this afternoon. It'll be just like that for your parents. Everything will be okay, you'll see."

"Do you really think so?" Haley asked anxiously.

"I do," Jill said.

Trisha McCoy was already on the ice when the five skaters from Silver Blades returned to the rink after lunch. Christopher Kane stood by the boards, watching her intently. He and Trisha and some of the other adults were scheduled to practice their scenes for the first time that afternoon.

As the tiny bells of the Sugarplum Fairy solo began to chime over the loudspeaker, Trisha smiled and glided through a series of spread-eagles, making a figure eight and raising her arms high above her head. Next she performed a few simple waltz jumps before picking up speed with crossovers into a triple flip–triple toe loop combination. She landed smoothly with her legs and arms fully extended.

Jill was enchanted as Trisha glided effortlessly across the length of the ice with her right leg extended in an arabesque. Then she flew right into a one-footed axel–triple salchow combination.

Trisha skated powerfully into a triple lutz, with a strongly held landing, before preparing for her next move. Effortlessly she performed a layback spin and whipped down into a sit spin. She closed by grabbing her right foot and pulling up into a leg mount spin. Exiting the spin, she executed a smooth footwork sequence, then moved into a beautiful spread-eagle with her hands folded across her chest. Her lovely green eyes were raised to the ceiling.

Jill thought it was one of the most beautiful performances she had ever seen. All the skaters at the boards broke into wild applause, and there were even a few shouts of "Bravo!" from the crew.

Trisha skated over to the side of the rink, right near where Jill and Tori were standing. Christopher kissed Trisha tenderly on the lips.

"You were perfect," he said to her.

"Thanks to you," Trisha purred back.

Tori, who was standing next to Jill, nudged her. "Look at that. I told you they'd make up," she said smugly. "Hey, Jill," Tori suddenly whispered. "Look over there. Isn't that Ludmila Petrova, from the Ice Academy? Come on, introduce me, okay?" Tori tried to drag Jill away.

"Wait a minute," Jill said. "I don't think this is the best time. Maybe later."

"What are you talking about?" Tori asked.

Jill lowered her voice. "I'm just not sure she wants to talk to *me*," she admitted. She didn't want to tell Tori that Ludmila hadn't asked her back to the Academy yet. "She didn't look at me once during practice this morning," Jill added.

"You're being silly," Tori said. "She probably just didn't see you. That's all."

"Maybe," Jill said.

Jill glanced across the ice. Amber had finished her warm-up. Now it was time for her to rehearse with Christopher Kane.

Christopher glided over to Amber and took her hand. He led her in a waltz around the rink, ending with a pull spiral. Christopher had a delighted smile on his face.

Jill glanced over at Ludmila, who was watching Amber intently. Jill saw Ludmila smile as Amber completed the spin. Christopher beamed down at her as well.

"They look really good together," Jill forced herself to say.

"Well, Ludmila seems to think so," Tori remarked. "I wonder if she'll ask Amber to the Academy someday."

Jill stared at Tori. She hadn't thought about that. What if Ludmila asked Amber to the Academy—not someday but now—instead of Jill? Everyone was always saying how talented Amber was. Now Ludmila could see it herself. Jill bit her lip. She watched as Ludmila followed Amber's every move.

Jill glanced around the rink. Everyone seemed impressed.

Then, suddenly, Jill spotted someone tall and good-looking standing by the bleachers. Ryan! She was so happy to see him.

"Hi," she said, hurrying over.

"Hi!" Ryan gave her a big smile. "This is totally amazing! You must be so excited, Jill. How has practice been going?"

Jill hesitated. She wanted to tell Ryan everything, but she didn't know where to begin.

Ryan was watching Christopher and Amber practice. "That Amber's a great skater, huh?" said Ryan, his voice full of admiration.

"What?" Jill said, surprised.

"I mean, anyone can see that she knows her stuff," he replied.

Jill swallowed. She couldn't exactly tell Ryan how she felt now. Complaining about Amber would come off as babyish and petty. "Yeah, she's very good," Jill said instead.

"Hey," Ryan said, gazing down at her. "You don't look very happy. What's wrong?"

"Everything!" Jill burst out, suddenly feeling close to tears. "I know it's wrong to feel this way, but watching Amber makes me feel terrible. I really wanted that role." Jill hung her head, ashamed.

Ryan put his arm around her. "C'mon, Jill, that's not so bad. Everyone gets jealous sometimes."

"Yeah, I know, but I wish I didn't," Jill said.

"If you're that upset, why not say something to Kathy?" Ryan suggested.

"I can't do that. It's unprofessional to complain," Jill said. "I'll just have to keep pretending that everything's okay, I guess."

"Hey, forget about Amber. Just skate your part and do your best, the way you always do."

"I will. Thanks, Ryan," Jill said.

"What are friends for?" Ryan asked with a sparkle in his brown eyes.

Jill had to smile when he looked at her that way.

"Listen, I have to get back to my cousins' house now. We're having a big family dinner," Ryan explained. "Will you have some free time tomorrow?"

"A little bit," Jill said. "We get a couple of hours off for lunch. But then it's right back here for dress rehearsal. I can't miss that."

"Well, a couple of hours leaves plenty of time for a special lunch together," Ryan said. "Would you like that?"

Jill hesitated. There was an awful lot to do the next

day. Going out for lunch might be cutting it really close. But there wasn't any other time Jill could have this kind of special date with Ryan. They would only be together in Boston this once. Jill made up her mind quickly.

"That'd be terrific," she said. "Can you come by about eleven-thirty?"

"No problem. It's a date. I'll see you then." Ryan gave Jill a quick squeeze before heading for the door.

A special date with Ryan! Jill smiled happily and thought, Tomorrow is going to be a big day.

9

Before breakfast the next morning Jill hurried to the wardrobe room. It had been set up in a corner room of the huge building. Jill had an appointment to try on the costume she would wear as the Dewdrop Fairy. She couldn't wait to see it.

The wardrobe room was crowded with costumes for *Nutcracker on Ice*. There were beautiful satin dresses with long, filmy skirts for the girls in the party scenes in act one. Two more racks were bulging with wispy chiffon dresses for the snowflakes and fairies in act two. The dresses glittered and gleamed with sequins and rhinestones in every color of the rainbow.

"Jill!" Tori rushed into the room. "Am I late? I have the first appointment." She stopped in surprise and gazed around. "Wow! This place is fantastic!" Tori exclaimed. "Can you believe all these beautiful outfits?"

"They look great," Jill agreed.

Amber entered the room. She walked around for a minute, admiring the costumes. Her hazel eyes were as big as saucers. She kept touching all the beading on the dresses.

"This is really amazing," Amber said to Jill. "I can't believe how pretty everything is. And fancy."

"Oh, my mom can make costumes like this," Tori bragged to Amber. "Even better. You haven't seen my fanciest skating outfits. I save them for competitions. But my closet is packed with them."

"Oh," Amber murmured. "I've never had a beautiful skating dress."

Amber looks a little sad, Jill thought. I guess I can understand how she feels. It's hard to compete with all the clothes Tori has.

A tall, slim woman came out of the tiny office to greet them. She had dark almond-shaped eyes. Her black hair was done in an elegant French twist, and she wore a stunning charcoal-gray dress with matching suede boots. A long measuring tape was draped around her neck. She wore a pincushion around one wrist like a bracelet.

"Hello, my name is Miko Yoshida," she told them. "Call me Miko. I'm the costumer for the show."

Tori, Jill, and Amber said hello.

"Please, find a place to sit down. Costume fitting doesn't take long. So be patient—I'll get to each of you quickly," Miko promised. She glanced at a list in her hand. "Tori Carsen is first," she said.

"That's me!" Tori raised her hand.

Miko smiled at her. "You're a mouse, right?"

"I'm the *lead* mouse," Tori declared.

"Right," Miko said. "I have something special for you. I'll be back in a jiffy." She disappeared between the racks of costumes.

"What do you mean, the *lead* mouse?" Jill asked Tori.

"Well, maybe not the lead," Tori admitted. "But I just found out—I've got a solo! It's in the scene where Clara falls asleep and the mice first come on the ice."

"But there isn't a solo in that scene," Jill said curiously.

"There wasn't one," Tori agreed. "But they thought my skating was so good that I deserved a special part. Dan came up with the idea. It turns out that he's an old friend of the choreographer."

"Good for you," Amber said. Tori ignored her.

"That's great," Jill commented.

Tori laughed. "Dan told me this was just the thing I needed. You know, to give me a boost with my positive thinking. I guess maybe he's not so bad after all."

"I never thought you'd say that," Jill said with a smile.

"I don't know why you don't like Dan," Amber said to Tori. "He's a really good coach. Though I'm awfully glad I get to work with Kathy."

Tori narrowed her eyes. Jill knew Tori was thinking that Amber had stolen Kathy's last coaching spot away from her. "I wonder what your outfit will look like," Jill remarked to Tori, trying to change the subject.

"Ugh. Like that!" Tori pointed.

Miko had just appeared holding a brownish-gray jumpsuit. Under her arm she held a big stuffed mouse head. The head had big ears, whiskers, and a bright polka-dot ribbon on top.

"All right, Tori—one lead mouse suit," Miko announced. "The bow is an extra touch, in honor of your solo."

Tori groaned. "How will I ever skate in that? The head is enormous! And the jumpsuit is so baggy!"

Miko laughed. "Well, it's not exactly glamorous. But you will be able to skate in it, you'll see. Just make sure to adjust the head so you can see out the bottom, under the nose."

Tori sighed. She ducked into the dressing area. When Tori came out, Miko made her bend and turn to see how the costume fit.

"Your coaches sent me all your measurements," Miko explained. "Your costumes will need only a quick tuck here and there." She took out a few pins and began fussing with the costume. "Oh, you're taller than I thought," she said.

"I had a little growth spurt," Tori told her. "Those measurements were taken several months ago. I'm a couple of inches taller now."

"Actually, that helps the suit fit better," Miko commented. "Now I'll take it in a little at the waist. We can show off *some* of your figure." The jumpsuit began to have a slimmer and more flattering shape.

"Tori, you look really cute," Jill said sincerely.

"I think it's adorable!" Amber squealed.

Tori spun around, admiring herself in the mirror. "It's not *so* bad," she admitted.

"Come in the back, Tori," Miko said. "I want to mark these adjustments with some tailor's chalk."

While they were gone, Bronya rushed in. "Jill, hi!" she called in surprise. "I'm glad you're here. We haven't had a chance to visit at all—in the rink, or at the hotel!"

"I know," Jill said. "So, how's everything going?"

"Great." Bronya grinned. "We're all having a wonderful time. Except for Ludmila," she added.

"Why?" Jill asked. "Isn't she happy with the show so far?"

"You know how she is," Bronya said.

"What do you mean?" Amber asked Bronya.

"Ludmila is very critical," Jill answered quickly, anxious to hear what Bronya would say.

"Well, Ludmila is happy with the producers," Bronya continued. "And she likes the hotel. She thinks the food's pretty good, too—especially the New England clam chowder. She says she wishes she could get it sent to her in Denver!"

"Um, has she said anything about the skating so far?" Jill asked.

"Not much," Bronya answered with a shrug. "She thinks that Christopher Kane and Trisha McCoy are wonderful. But Ludmila admires professionals, you know."

"Was Ludmila a professional skater?" Amber asked Jill.

"She trained some of the skaters in the Olympics," Jill answered, a little impatiently.

Amber turned to Bronya. "It's really hard to get invited to the Academy, isn't it?"

"Yes, it is," Bronya replied.

"Do they look for anything special?" Amber asked.

"Why are you asking so many questions?" Jill burst out. "Do you want to go there?"

"Of course," Amber said matter-of-factly. "Doesn't everyone?"

Jill stared at Amber. It's not enough for her to come to Silver Blades and take the role of Clara, Jill thought. Now she wants to go to the Academy, too!

Miko hurried back to where they were waiting. "Jill Wong," she read from her list.

"That's me," Jill answered.

"You're the Dewdrop Fairy. You're lucky, Jill. I have a lovely dress for you." Miko went to one of the costume racks.

When Jill saw the costume in Miko's hands, she gasped. The dress was a bright emerald-green satin. The neckline and the puff sleeves were trimmed in delicate green lace. The hem was scalloped, with two layers of ruffles. Brilliant silver sequins were sewn all over the front of the dress in a pattern that reminded Jill of drops of water.

"Is that really what I'm going to wear?" Jill asked.

"Isn't it lovely?" Miko beamed with pride. "I worked hard on this one. I thought you'd be happy. Let's try it on you."

Miko helped Jill slip into the dress. Jill gazed at herself in the mirror. She felt like a fairy princess! She gave a twirl, and the layers of ruffles swirled around her.

"Wow!" Amber exclaimed. "You look amazing!"

"I wish *I* had a dress like that," Tori complained.

"Why, it's almost a perfect fit," Miko said in surprise. "Just one simple adjustment." She bent and marked the waist with her pins. "I guess this costume was meant for you, Jill."

"You look so beautiful, Jill," Bronya said in admiration.

"Okay, Jill, better take it off," said Miko. "You won't need to wear it until the dress rehearsal this afternoon."

Jill glanced in the mirror one last time before she headed back to the dressing area. She never wanted to take off the beautiful costume.

When Jill came back out wearing her leggings and red T-shirt, Bronya turned to her.

"Hey, Jill, Marie and I are having lunch with Ludmila today. Do you want to come along?" Bronya asked. "It would be a good chance for us to get together. Like old times."

"Great!" Jill said. She could tell Ludmila how hard she'd been working. Ludmila might even invite Jill back to the Academy right at lunch! But then Jill remembered Ryan. She'd promised to have lunch with him. And she didn't have a phone number where she could call him and change their plans.

Jill wondered for an instant if she could go with Bronya without telling Ryan. He'd understand, wouldn't he? Or maybe she could bring Ryan along with her! No, Jill told herself, that would be a disaster.

"Bronya, I'm sorry," Jill finally said. "I can't go with you. I forgot—I already made a lunch date."

"Oh, I'm sorry, too," Bronya told her. Miko called Bronya in for her fitting then, and Bronya said good-bye.

What bad luck, Jill thought miserably. That lunch could have been my best chance to talk to Ludmila. Jill turned to leave the costume room.

"Jill, wait!" Amber cried. "I'm next. Don't you want to stay and see *my* costume?"

Jill gaped at Amber for a moment. "No, thanks," she managed to say. She turned away. Did Amber really think Jill wanted to see her dressed up in the Clara costume? That was just about the last thing Jill ever wanted to do.

When Jill stepped out of the wardrobe room, Monique Descartes was standing nearby.

"Jill!" Monique called when she spotted Jill. "May I speak to you, please?"

10

"**G**ood morning, Jill," Monique greeted her warmly. "I hope you don't mind my asking, but did you get a chance to look over our brochure? I'd like to know what you think."

"I thought the school looked wonderful," Jill said truthfully. "In fact, when I called my parents last night I told them all about it. They were pretty impressed."

Monique smiled. "Well, then, we should do something about that. Jeanne and I have time reserved for our skaters at the Soldiers Field Memorial Rink this afternoon. Maybe you could meet us there and show us more of your skating."

"You mean you want me to audition for you?" Jill asked.

"Yes. Very much." Monique wrote down the name of the rink on a slip of paper. "You don't have to make up your mind about the school right now. Just come if you can. We would love to see you." Monique handed Jill the paper and said good-bye.

Jill stared at the paper in her hand. When she looked up she noticed that Amber was hurrying out of the wardrobe room toward the ice. Amber quickly put on her skates and began her warm-up.

Jill also laced her skates and headed for the ice. She wouldn't decide anything right then. She needed to practice her back camel spin. It didn't quite have the polish she wanted.

Jill performed the spin a few times. She was about to try it again when she noticed Kathy watching her.

"Time to move on, Jill," Kathy called to her. "Try your triple salchow–double toe loop combo followed by the sit spin."

Jill felt as if Kathy was giving up on the back camel spin—and on her. She could barely look at her coach. Quickly she bent over and tightened her laces, hiding her face. Kathy used to say nice things about my skating, Jill thought. But that was before Amber came along.

Straightening up, Jill saw Christopher Kane gliding across the ice directly toward her. Jill stared.

"Hello, I'm Christopher," he said, stopping in front of Jill and Kathy. His brown eyes twinkled. "I wanted to say hello."

"Hi," Jill said, hoping she didn't sound too nervous. "I'm Jill Wong."

"Oh, I know who you are, Jill," Christopher said. "I've been watching you."

"You have?" Jill almost squeaked. Christopher Kane had been watching *her*? What did that mean?

"Hi, Christopher, I'm Kathy Bart," said Jill's coach. "I saw you skate in the *Ice Rocks* show last year. I really enjoyed your routine."

"Oh, thanks," said Christopher. "That was a fun show. You must be very proud of Jill. She's quite a skater. Trisha and I are both very impressed by her."

Jill couldn't believe her ears. She glanced quickly around the rink. If only Ludmila could hear this! Jill felt her cheeks glowing.

"Silver Blades must be a very special skating club," Christopher continued. He pointed in Amber's direction. "Look at her—so young and already so talented."

Jill felt her smile fade. Amber again!

"Amber is our newest member," Kathy said proudly. "She's exceptional. But then, I think our whole club is something special."

"Well, time for me to get back to work," Christopher said. "I just wanted to say hi." He glided away, giving a little wave. "See you around. Keep up the good work."

As Christopher skated off, he also waved to Amber.

"Well, that was nice of him, wasn't it?" Kathy asked Jill with a smile on her face.

"Yeah," Jill answered quietly. "I guess so." She couldn't help feeling down. Amber's name was *always* being mentioned.

"Jill, what is it?" Kathy asked with concern. "Is something wrong? You don't seem very happy."

Jill stared down at her skates. Kathy was right. She didn't feel happy at all.

"I just can't help it, Kathy," Jill burst out. "Amber gets to star as Clara and skate with Trisha and Christopher—and I don't."

"That's not a very professional attitude, Jill," Kathy said with a disapproving shake of her head.

"I know," Jill admitted. "But I just don't understand. I worked really hard. And I skated really well at the auditions. I know I did!"

Kathy nodded. "That's true, Jill. But don't you think you should focus on how well things are going for you, instead of worrying about whether or not anyone is doing better than you?"

"I guess," Jill mumbled.

"So you're not the star of the show—this time," Kathy said in her no-nonsense manner. "But being the star is not what's important. Skating your best is." Kathy softened her tone. "Now, let's really nail this Dewdrop Fairy routine."

Jill nodded and glided over to her start position. "Focus," she whispered under her breath. She began the Dewdrop Fairy program again, gliding through the crossovers and jumps without a mistake. She felt terrific. She went from one move to another with no effort at all. It was the best she had skated in weeks. She was actually disappointed when she came to the end of her routine. She paused for a moment before gliding over to Kathy.

"Much better, Jill," Kathy said. "I think you're really improving."

"Thanks, Kathy," Jill managed to say. But she felt disappointed again. Couldn't Kathy see how well she had skated? Jill was sure she wasn't just imagining it. Then why didn't her coach say so?

Jill glanced up and spotted Amber on the other side of the rink. The young skater was talking to Ludmila.

For a moment Jill felt as if her heart had stopped. Ludmila was gesturing as she spoke. Amber seemed to be listening intently, and she nodded frequently.

Jill swallowed hard. Was Amber asking Ludmila about going to the Academy? Ludmila was acting so friendly. Jill couldn't stand it. Maybe the Paris school was the best answer to her problems. Jill squared her shoulders. I *will* audition for them today, she decided right then.

Kathy tapped Jill on the shoulder, interrupting her thoughts. "Jill, were you listening to me?"

"What?" Jill asked, surprised. "I was just thinking about something. Uh—my lunch date with Ryan. Remember, I'm meeting him soon."

"That's right. Well, since you've done so much this morning, why don't we stop now?" Kathy suggested. "Lunch is in a few minutes anyway. I'll be working with Amber when you get back this afternoon. From two to four, until the dress rehearsal. But you can use that time to practice on your own. You'll be fine. Okay?"

"Okay." Jill hesitated. "Oh, Kathy, I—" She was about to tell Kathy about being asked to audition for the Paris Ice School, but Kathy interrupted.

"Sorry, Jill. I need to catch Amber," Kathy said. "You hurry and change. I'll see you later."

Jill skated to the side of the rink and slipped on her skate guards. She didn't really have time to talk to Kathy anyway. Ryan would be there in just a few minutes. Jill rushed into the dressing room and changed into black jeans and a red mohair sweater. She smiled as she pulled the sweater on. She had worn it on her very first date with Ryan.

She quickly redid her braid and turned to leave. Just as she was walking out the door she ran into Tori.

"Hey, Jill," Tori greeted her. "You look great. Going to your big lunch date, right? Have fun!"

"Thanks, I will," Jill said.

Ryan was already waiting in his car in the parking lot. Jill climbed into the front seat beside him.

"I thought we'd go to Fisherman's Wharf," Ryan said. "They have great seafood restaurants there."

The place they chose was cozy and old-fashioned. The walls were covered with dark paneling. Fishing nets hung from the ceiling, and all kinds of antique lanterns hung on the walls. The overhead lights were made from old captain's wheels. There was even a gigantic anchor next to the fireplace, where a roaring fire was burning.

Jill gazed around at everything in delight. She and

Ryan held hands until the waitress brought their lunch.

"Mmm, this is delicious!" Jill exclaimed, tasting her clam chowder. "And I've finally seen something of Boston—besides the rink and the hotel."

"You've been working really hard, huh?" Ryan asked.

"Really hard," Jill said. "There's a lot of pressure not to make any mistakes. After all, it *is* national TV." She glanced down at her napkin. "Ryan, there's something that I haven't told anybody," she confided. "Can you keep a secret?"

"Sure," Ryan said.

"I've been invited to audition for the International Ice School of Paris," Jill told him. "It was a big surprise. And also a real honor. The school is very famous."

"Wow, I'm impressed," Ryan said. "But I thought you wanted to go back to the Ice Academy in Denver."

"I do," Jill admitted. "Only Ludmila hasn't invited me back. So I thought I'd better audition for the Paris school."

Ryan frowned. "Well, suppose you *do* get in. How will I ever see you if you're training in Paris?"

"Let's not worry about that now," Jill said.

"Sure—we can work something out," Ryan said in a more cheerful voice. "Besides, I bet Ludmila asks you back. You're such a great skater. Why wouldn't she want you back in Denver?"

Jill flushed. "Thanks, Ryan. I really appreciate that."

But Jill wasn't as certain as Ryan. After all, Ryan didn't really know that much about skating, and he hadn't seen how Ludmila acted around Amber.

"I can audition today at two o'clock," Jill told Ryan. "But I'm supposed to practice on my own this afternoon, from two to four. And then we have our big dress rehearsal."

"How long do you think this audition will take?" Ryan asked.

Jill shrugged. "Less than half an hour, probably."

"Then what's the problem?" Ryan asked. "I'll pick you up at the rink at two and drive you to the audition. I'll wait and drive you back to the rink afterward."

"That's great!" Jill paused. "Of course, I'm supposed to tell Kathy or Dan where I'm going," she added. "But what if they won't let me leave? They might think I'll be late for dress rehearsal."

"That's not until four," Ryan pointed out. "You'll be back in plenty of time. I bet no one will even notice you were gone."

Jill was convinced. She dug the slip of paper out of her pocket. "Well, here's the name of the rink," she said, handing the paper to Ryan.

"Great. I can get directions from my cousins," Ryan said. "Don't worry about anything. It'll be easy."

Jill breathed a sigh of relief. "Thanks, Ryan. You really saved my life."

After lunch, about twelve-thirty, Ryan drove Jill back to the Boston Skate Club. Two o'clock came faster than Jill had expected. She had already packed her gear into her plaid skate bag. Luckily, no one she knew was in the dressing room. Amber and Kathy were already back on the ice, and Haley and Patrick had just started to warm up. Jill walked quickly toward the door, hoping that no one would notice her sneaking out.

Suddenly she heard a voice behind her.

"Hey, Jill, where are you going?" It was Tori.

Jill whipped around. "Um, I'm just going outside for a moment," she fibbed. "I need to take a walk." She felt bad about lying to Tori. But Ryan was right. Jill would be back before anyone even noticed she was gone.

"Okay, see you," Tori said with a wave.

Jill hurried outside and crossed the parking lot to Ryan's car. Just then a taxi pulled up. Christopher and Trisha were inside. Jill sucked in her breath. Christopher was looking right in her direction.

Jill ran the rest of the way, pulled open the door to Ryan's car, and jumped into the front seat. "It's Christopher Kane," she said breathlessly. "I hope he didn't see me!"

"Duck down," Ryan said.

Jill slid down in the seat. Her heart was pounding. As Ryan pulled out of the parking lot, Jill peeked out the side window. The taxi had already gone. The doors to the arena were closed. And Christopher Kane was nowhere in sight.

11

Jill turned to Ryan. "What if Christopher saw us?"

Ryan glanced at Jill as he pulled out into traffic. "What if he did? You're only going out for a few minutes."

"I guess so," Jill answered. "But I still hope he doesn't tell anyone."

"Hey, he's probably got more important things on his mind," Ryan said.

Jill gazed at Ryan thoughtfully. "You're right," she agreed. "He's a big star. Why would he care about where I am?"

"Right. So don't worry. Just think about skating your absolute best."

Jill smiled at Ryan gratefully. "*You're* the absolute best," she told him.

The Soldiers Field Memorial Rink was a large, round

steel-blue building. Ryan parked the car in the lot, and the two of them hurried into the building together.

Monique and Jeanne were standing right by the entrance. Jill grabbed Ryan's arm and pulled him over to them.

"Jill!" Monique exclaimed. "You did come! Good."

"Hi, Monique. Hi, Jeanne," Jill greeted them. "This is Ryan McKensey. He's a friend from Seneca Hills. He drove me over here."

"How nice that your friend is here in Boston, Jill."

"Jill," Monique said, "if you are ready, the rink is ours right now."

Jill nodded. "I'm ready."

"I guess I'll wait in the snack bar over there," Ryan said.

"That'd be great," Jill told him. "See you later."

Ryan gave Jill a thumbs-up sign and waved. Jill waved back.

Jill followed Monique and Jeanne as they headed for the ice.

"Ryan seems like a nice boy," Monique commented.

"He is. He's really been a good friend," Jill replied with a trace of shyness.

"Friends are so important," Jeanne said seriously. "I'm sure you make friends easily wherever you go, Jill. Isn't that so?"

"I guess." Jill started thinking. It hadn't been easy for her to make friends when she first got to Denver. In fact, for a long time Jill had thought that Bronya was cold and unfriendly. It had taken her a while to see that

Bronya was only shy. And Jill had had some trouble fitting in with the new crowd at the beginning.

For the first time Jill wondered if this was really a good idea. How would she get along with the students in Paris? She already knew that it wasn't easy making a brand-new start in a new place. And she didn't speak any French.

"Um, what are the students like in Paris?" Jill asked Monique.

"They're very nice. Very serious," Monique said.

"Of course, they are so busy with their skating," Jeanne added, "they don't have much time for socializing. I'm sure you know how it is, Jill."

Jill remembered what Bronya had said over the phone: practice, practice, practice. Jill smiled. "That's okay," she commented. "I'm used to hard work."

"It isn't *all* work," Jeanne said. "We try to have some fun. There are often small parties where everyone gets together. It's very nice."

"That *is* nice," Jill agreed.

Monique gave a little laugh. "Sometimes it is quite funny to see everyone trying to communicate. After all, not everyone speaks French."

Jill swallowed hard. "I don't know any French," she admitted. "How would I be coached? How would I talk to anyone?"

"Oh, don't worry. You will pick it up quickly," Jeanne assured her. "And your coach would speak English."

"There are many, many people who speak English," Monique added.

They reached the ice. Jill saw it gleaming. A Zamboni was just finishing its rounds.

"We were lucky to be able to book this time," Monique explained. "The lockers are over there. We'll wait for you here."

"Thanks. I'll be right back." Jill flew into the locker room. She changed into her red velour top and black velvet leggings. She really wanted to look good for this audition. If you're going to do something, do it right, her father had said to her the night before. Her mother had agreed. They both thought Jill should audition for the Paris school if she was given the chance. But they had warned her not to make any decisions without them. Jill was supposed to call them back that night with any new development.

Jill was glad she had called her parents. They were really supportive of her. But there were so many problems to work out. Jill knew it would be expensive to fly all the way to Paris. Much more expensive than flying to Denver. She wondered what her parents really thought about that—and what they thought about her possibly living so far away.

When would she see her family? She'd only been away from home a few days, and she already missed her brothers and sisters. And her parents, Jill admitted to herself.

And then there was Ryan. When—how—would she ever get to see him?

But I haven't really decided to go there yet, she reminded herself. And now is *not* the time to worry about it.

Jill hurried onto the ice. She handed her music tape to the man in the sound booth. Then she warmed up quickly. She had decided to skate the Clara role. She had worked hard on it for the ice show audition. And the coaches had already seen her do her Dewdrop Fairy routine. Besides, Jill wanted *someone* to know that she could skate the lead part well—as well as Amber.

The music began. Jill felt a familiar thrill as she imagined herself as Clara. She took off in a triple toe loop and landed smoothly. It felt great to have the big rink all to herself. Jill lifted into a perfect double axel and landed smoothly again. She spun into a flying camel, then sped across the gleaming ice in a series of backward crossovers. Easily she glided into the final double Lutz–double loop combination.

She was really enjoying herself, and she knew it showed. This was how she had skated in Seneca Hills. She felt as if she *were* Clara, and the difficult moves were easy for her.

Jill finished with a layback. She paused, letting herself enjoy the satisfaction of having done a really good job. Then she glided to the side of the rink.

"Excellent, just excellent." Monique's eyes were glowing as she praised Jill.

"Very impressive," Jeanne agreed. "Beautiful work."

Jill beamed at them. She knew she had done well.

"If you don't mind, Jill, we'd like to see your triple

flip–double loop. And perhaps you could follow that with a change-foot sit spin and a spread-eagle?"

"Sure thing," Jill replied.

She circled the rink a few times. Then she lifted into the air, bringing her arms in close and maintaining a straight spine to streamline her body. Landing with precision, she took off again. She performed the change-foot sit spin, which she had been working on as part of the Dewdrop Fairy solo. She finished with a weaving spread-eagle sequence.

"Jill, your skating is simply beautiful," Monique declared. "Why don't you go ahead and change? We can discuss details later."

"Congratulations," Jeanne added. "You are a most talented young lady."

"Thanks very much," Jill told them. "I loved skating for you. I'll be back in a minute."

As Jill changed, her mind was racing. She was thrilled that Monique and Jeanne had admired her skating. But something else was also on her mind.

Jill came back out and sat with Monique and Jeanne on the bleachers.

"Well, perhaps we should tell you a bit more about our school," Monique said. "We're right outside Paris. It's very pretty, very near the River Seine. It is not too far from the airport, so it is easy to fly back and forth to the United States."

"Isn't that expensive, though?" Jill asked. "I mean, my family doesn't have a whole lot of money."

"That is a concern," Monique agreed. "Some of our

foreign students stay during the holidays. They need to save money. It can be hard at first. But we are like a little family. Everyone is quite close."

"You would get used to it," Jeanne assured her. "It is lovely to spend holidays in Paris."

Jill frowned. What would it be like to spend Christmas without her family? And in a foreign country?

It was hard enough for Jill to be in Boston with Christmas so near. What if she couldn't get home from Paris for next Christmas? There would be no writing the family letter to Santa. No reading *The Nutcracker* out loud to Henry, Kristi, Randi, Michael, Mark, and Laurie. It seemed awful.

"Well," Jill said slowly, "I know that a skating career requires sacrifices. Maybe this would be a good thing for me." Especially if Ludmila doesn't want me back, she added silently.

"Of course, you'll have to think it over carefully. We understand what a big decision this is. You would want to talk to your parents first. But we must tell you that we are considering another skater for our school. And we have only one space right now."

Jill saw the two women exchange looks.

She wondered if the other skater was Amber. She bet it was. After all, how could the coaches not have noticed Amber? She was skating the lead.

"I'm so glad we were able to see you skate, Jill. Think about everything we've said. And speak to your parents, too," Monique urged.

"I will," Jill agreed. If Amber decided to go to the

Paris school, that might mean Jill could have her spot in Denver. But that wasn't the way Jill wanted it to be. Jill wanted to be Ludmila's first choice.

Jill said good-bye to Monique and Jeanne. She met Ryan outside the snack bar, and they hurried back to his car. Jill was silent on the ride to the Boston Skate Club rink. She stared out the window at the unfamiliar streets. This is what it feels like to be away from home, Jill reminded herself. She glanced over at Ryan and thought about how much it would hurt to be so far away from him.

"Are you all right?" he asked.

"I was just thinking that Paris is awfully far away."

"It sure is," Ryan said.

Jill swallowed hard. Going back to Denver was one thing. She and Ryan could call each other. And she could visit. But what if she went to Paris? Would she and Ryan have to break up?

Finally Ryan pulled into the parking lot of the rink. He stopped the car and turned to Jill.

"Listen, Jill, you have to do whatever's right for you," he said.

"I know," Jill said softly.

"Hey!" Ryan suddenly laughed. "Maybe I could transfer to Paris to finish high school!"

Jill laughed, too. "I don't think so."

"Guess not," Ryan said lightly. He leaned over and gave her a kiss.

Jill jumped out of the car and waved good-bye. She pulled open the heavy door of the rink.

The minute she got inside, Bronya came running up to her. Jill noticed that Bronya was already wearing her costume.

"Where *were* you?" Bronya asked Jill urgently. "There was a change in the schedule. We've started the dress rehearsal. Everyone was looking for you." Bronya gave her a sympathetic look. "I think you're in big trouble."

"Oh, no," Jill said. "Thanks for the warning."

She raced toward the dressing room, pulling off her red parka as she went. She was halfway there when Christopher Kane appeared. He blocked her path, shaking his finger at her.

"Here's the missing skater!" he announced loudly.

Several people turned to see what the fuss was about.

"I saw you sneaking off with your boyfriend," Christopher continued. He shook his head and raised his eyes, giving a dramatic sigh. "Ah, romance! The pain of being in love!" Christopher grinned. "But it's worth it, isn't it?" He winked at her and strode away, whistling loudly.

A few people laughed. Others just stared. Jill felt as though her cheeks were on fire. She wished she could disappear.

Then Kathy hurried over to her. Her hands were on her hips, and her blue eyes were flashing with anger.

"How could you, Jill?" Kathy scolded. "You know you were supposed to tell Dan or me if you went anywhere. It was irresponsible of you. And your behavior reflects badly on Silver Blades. You're here to skate, not visit with your boyfriend. Am I making myself clear?"

Jill nodded miserably. She felt horrible. And angry. Kathy didn't have to yell at her in front of everyone. That was really unfair!

"Go get changed," Kathy snapped. "At least we didn't rehearse your scene yet."

Jill was humiliated. She turned toward the dressing room—and saw Ludmila standing a few feet away. Ludmila had heard everything!

12

Jill opened her eyes and stretched. Tori was still asleep in the other bed. Jill rolled over and gazed out the window of the hotel room. There was a funny, nervous feeling in her stomach. Then she remembered—today was the big day, the taping of *Nutcracker on Ice*!

A moment later there was a knock on the door.

"Mmm, who's that?" Tori asked. Sleepily she turned over.

"I'll see." Jill threw on her bathrobe and hurried to the door. It was Haley.

"Hi, you guys," Haley said excitedly. "I have the best news. Wait till you hear! My dad's coming to the show!"

"Oh, wow!" Tori yelled, jumping out of bed. "The show! It's today! Come on, we have to get ready!"

Jill glanced at the bedside clock. "Relax, Tori. We've got plenty of time. We don't have to be there for two more hours." But she couldn't blame Tori for being excited. She was, too. Jill turned to Haley. "What's this about your dad?"

"He decided to come and surprise me," Haley said happily. "Isn't that great? I'm going to get him a pass so he can be in the audience."

"That's great," Jill told Haley. Jill knew it would be nice for Haley to have her father cheering her on.

Jill thought of Ryan, who would also be sitting in the audience. She shivered in anticipation. She couldn't wait for him to see *Nutcracker on Ice*.

The dress rehearsal the day before had been incredible. At first Jill had been so upset that she'd thought she would never be able to skate her role. But she'd soon realized no one was thinking about what had happened to her. No one mentioned Christopher's teasing or Kathy's scolding. And Jill soon forgot those incidents, too.

The ice rink had been transformed for the dress rehearsal. The colored lights made the sets look magical. And the costumes made everyone look so glamorous!

Then, when the skating had begun, Jill had forgotten all her worries. She couldn't take her eyes off Christopher. His skating was more expressive than ever. Everyone he skated with seemed to give their best.

They had run straight through act one without stopping. There had been hardly any mistakes. And even though it was only a dress rehearsal, everyone had burst into wild applause at the end. Act two had been more of a blur to Jill. She was so nervous that she couldn't pay much attention to anyone else. It felt as if she waited forever to skate her part. When her turn came she performed very well. She made no major mistakes, either. Still, she was a little disappointed. She had wanted to feel a special spark as she skated. That hadn't happened. Jill hoped that the actual show would be different. She wanted to skate the performance of her life.

The next two hours flew by. By the time the shuttle bus pulled up to the rink, all the skaters were keyed up—excited and nervous at the same time.

"Look at the lines," Jill murmured.

A long line of people stood waiting to get into the taping. Jill and the others hurried inside the rink. The crew was already there. Everyone bustled around looking important. They adjusted the cameras and made final changes to the sets. A special seating section was marked off for the audience.

Bronya ran up to Jill with a concerned look on her face.

"Have you heard the news?" she asked Jill nervously.

"No, what?" Jill replied.

"Trisha and Christopher had another huge fight last night," she answered. "They might not skate today."

"No way! Who told you that?" Jill asked in amazement.

"Marie overheard one of the producers on his cellular phone," Bronya explained. "He was really upset. Everyone's talking about it."

Tori rushed up to the two girls. She looked pale.

"Can you believe it?" Tori asked Jill. "Do you think it's true? Everyone's saying that Trisha and Christopher broke up last night! They say the whole show is off!"

"It can't be! Let's wait and see what happens," Jill said. "Maybe everything will work out."

But Jill wasn't as calm as she sounded. She was worried, too. Haley and Patrick joined the group of skaters standing near the boards. Even Patrick seemed concerned.

"I hope it's not true," he said. "We worked hard on this show. It would be terrible if they canceled it."

The doors of the rink flew open. Everyone turned and stared. It was Trisha and Christopher! They were smiling and holding hands.

"Greetings, all!" Christopher cried out. "Another happy day. Is everybody ready to skate?"

Jill heaved a sigh of relief.

"Well, so much for that," Haley remarked with a shrug. "I guess even those two know that the show must go on."

"Hey, look, Haley." Jill nudged her friend. "There's your dad!"

Haley gave a whoop and ran to give her father a hug. Jill grinned at Patrick.

"That was a really nice surprise for her," Jill remarked.

"She's so happy to see her dad," Patrick said. "You know how worried she's been about her parents. I hope this visit goes well for her."

"Me too," Jill said. As she turned to go into the dressing room, she spotted Ryan standing by the bleachers. "Ryan!" she called. Ryan saw her and gave a wave. Jill waved back.

"Can't talk now," she told him. "I've got to get dressed!"

"See you later," Ryan called back. He gave her a thumbs-up sign. "And good luck!"

Jill's costume was already inside the dressing room. Each time she saw it she was thrilled by how beautiful it was. And, thanks to Miko, it was comfortable, too. When she had worn it in the dress rehearsal, the costume had moved as if it were a part of her.

"It sure beats being a mouse," Jill said out loud. She giggled to herself. "For once in my life I have a better outfit than Tori!"

There was a list posted beside the dressing room. It told when each skater would have his or her hair and makeup done. Jill saw that Amber was already seated at a special table. A professional makeup artist had finished getting Amber ready for the cameras. Now the hairstylist was brushing out the younger girl's hair.

Jill had a long wait for her turn. She sat down and began to undo her French braid.

"Wait!" Amber cried. She pointed right at Jill. "That's how I want my hair done," Amber told the hairstylist, whose name was Kelly.

Jill looked up, startled.

"Sorry," Kelly told Amber. "You have to wear your hair down." She held up a headpiece trimmed with sparkling rhinestones. "That looks best with this tiara," the stylist explained.

Amber pouted. "I really wanted my hair like Jill's," she complained. "Maybe you just don't know how to do a braid like that," she said to Kelly.

"It's wrong for you," Kelly insisted.

"I don't care," Amber said. "It's what I want."

Jill shook her head. Amber was impossible. Jill just couldn't put up with her anymore. She went over to Amber's table.

"Stop acting like a prima donna!" Jill said. "Kelly just told you why you should wear your hair down. Why don't you listen to her?"

Jill saw tears well up in Amber's eyes. "You're so *mean* to me," Amber cried. "Why?"

"Because you're pushy," Jill shot back angrily. "All the time."

Kelly seemed embarrassed. A few of the other girls in the dressing room turned to stare. Jill felt her cheeks burning. She knew she was making a scene, but she couldn't stop herself.

"What's your problem, anyway?" she whispered to Amber.

Amber blinked back her tears. "I was just trying to be friendly. But I don't even know why I wanted to be friends with you." Amber sounded really hurt. "I guess I'm just stupid. You always make me feel left out. You act like you hate me!"

They were really attracting attention now, but Jill still couldn't stop.

"And what about you, Amber? You always follow me around. You ask a million nosy questions. On top of that, you're always trying to take things away from me!" Jill was trembling with anger. "Don't pretend you don't."

"That's not true!" Tears spilled down Amber's cheeks. "All I ever heard was what a great skater you are. But you're mean! I don't know why I thought you were so great."

Jill stared at Amber. "You thought I was great?" she blurted. She didn't know what to say.

"Of course," Amber said. She wiped her face. "You're the best skater in Silver Blades. You were picked to go to the Academy. And you're really pretty, and you have tons of friends and a really cute boyfriend."

"Is *that* why you've been following me around? And asking me all those questions?" Jill's voice softened.

"Sure," said Amber. "How else could I learn to be like you?"

Kathy stuck her head in the door. "Hey—what's going on in here? Where is everyone? It's showtime!"

Amber rushed to her locker. With Miko's help, she changed into her Clara costume.

It was Jill's turn for hair and makeup. Kelly pulled Jill's black hair away from her face into an elegant twist. Then Jill slipped on her costume and checked herself in the mirror. Her cheeks were pink, and her eyes sparkled. The dress fit like a dream.

Soon it will be time to skate the best performance of your life, Jill told herself. She hurried out of the dressing room and into the hallway, where Dan was waiting with his camera.

"Jill, say cheese!" Dan called.

Jill paused, and Dan snapped her picture. "Another piece of Silver Blades history," he told her.

Silver Blades history, Jill repeated to herself. She thought back to all the good times she had had in Silver Blades. She thought of all her hard work over the years—and of the great friends she'd made.

Kathy hurried to her side. "Jill, you look wonderful," her coach said, giving her a hug. "I know you'll be fantastic out there."

"You do?" Jill asked.

"Of course!" Kathy said, puzzled. "Don't you know that?"

Jill bit her lip. "Well, I didn't want to say anything, but you were acting like you thought I *didn't* skate well anymore."

"I was?" Kathy looked bewildered. "You know I push skaters hard, Jill. But I always have. If anything, I thought *you* weren't being very fair to yourself."

"What do you mean?" It was Jill's turn to be puzzled.

"You've been acting like your part isn't important. But it is. The Dewdrop Fairy is a great role," Kathy said. "I thought you knew that. It was supposed to be given to a professional skater. Then the producer and the scouts saw your audition. They were so impressed that they decided to give you the part instead."

"Really?" Jill began to feel a lot better. "I didn't know that. Why didn't you tell me?"

"I didn't think I had to!" Kathy exclaimed. "I know the part of Clara is long. But I thought you could see that your part is much harder. A younger skater could never carry it off. But you can do it—and do it well."

"Then you never thought my skating was getting weak?"

"Never!" Kathy laughed. "Oh, Jill, I'm sorry! I had no idea you felt this way. We should have talked a lot sooner."

Jill reached out to Kathy and hugged her tightly. "We talked just in time," she said. "Thanks, Kathy. I feel a lot better!"

"I guess there's something else I should have told you before," Kathy said, looking a little embarrassed. "I'm really proud of you, Jill." She hugged Jill back. "Good luck out there."

Jill felt as if she was about to cry.

With her head held high, Jill walked to the rink to wait for her turn to warm up. She felt happier than she had in weeks.

Do your best, she told herself firmly. After all, it's time to make history for Silver Blades.

13

Finally it was time for Jill to skate the Dewdrop Fairy solo. Jill glided to the center of the rink. Blue and white spotlights came on. The sets looked magical. Jill felt as if she were really surrounded by snow-covered trees. And she felt like a fairy princess. Taking a deep breath, Jill cleared her mind. Her warm-up had left her eager to skate. She felt a thrill as she raised her arms to her starting pose.

The music began with the chiming of bells and the singing of violins. Jill balanced on the points of her skates. Happiness filled her as she began her routine. The layers of her ruffled skirt floated around her like a cloud. She glided easily into the back camel spin.

The music grew louder, and more instruments joined in. Jill arched her back and reached behind her to catch hold of her left skate. It felt so easy! She completed four rotations, finished the spin, and began the front crossovers leading into her next set of waltz jumps.

Making a half turn, she performed a series of backward crossovers. It was time for her first difficult combination, the triple flip–double Lutz. Her takeoff was perfect and her landing flawless. The audience burst into applause.

Jill noticed the cameras following her as she crossed the ice. She knew the smile on her face was a real one. She took another turn around the ice and realized she felt that spark of something special. Suddenly she *was* the Dewdrop Fairy—a light and delicate creature.

She performed a precise change-foot sit spin, then flew into the triple salchow–double toe loop. It came so easily, she couldn't believe it. She felt as if she were enchanted.

After performing several more difficult moves with virtually no effort, Jill completed a perfect sit spin. Her arms reached forward and up, bringing her to a standing position. Then she performed an elegant layback. It was the final spin in her solo. Her dress twirled around her like a flower. She moved into the dramatic finish and closed her eyes before fanning out her hands on either side of her face. When she looked up, the camera was focused on her smile.

Applause broke out from the audience and the crew.

Jill knew it was the best performance of her life. The audience gave her another round of applause.

As she glided to the side of the rink and stepped off the ice, Ryan ran up and grabbed her hand.

"You were fantastic," he whispered, giving Jill a hug.

"Thanks," Jill murmured. "I'm so glad you were here."

Dan came up. "How about a picture of you two for the scrapbook?"

Jill and Ryan looked at each other. Then Ryan put his arm around Jill. She snuggled up to him and smiled. "Now I'll never forget how I feel today."

Dan snapped the picture.

"That was great, guys," Dan said. "I think it's going to be an especially nice photo, if I do say so myself."

Jill laughed and gave Ryan a quick kiss. Then she noticed Amber watching them from the railing. She knew Amber's Clara solos were coming up again. They were taping all the solos a second time. That way they would have extra footage for the final edited tape. In fact, it was the solo that all the singles skaters had learned to audition for the show. Only now Jill didn't care that she hadn't gotten the part. She just felt bad that she had lost her temper with Amber earlier. Not that the other girl was suddenly going to become a friend, but at least Jill understood why Amber had acted the way she had. Quickly Jill left Ryan and went over to the younger skater.

"Look, Amber," Jill began, "I'm sorry we argued. Let's just say we both could have acted differently from the beginning."

Amber was silent. "I guess that's true," she finally

said. "And just so you know, I think you were a beautiful Dewdrop Fairy."

"Thanks," Jill said. "Now it's your turn again. Knock 'em dead!"

Amber smiled and skated onto the ice. Her costume was white lace trimmed with tiny pearls and sequins. It was much sweeter and more girlish than Jill's. Jill pulled Ryan closer to the rink so they could see the ice more clearly.

Amber took her position in the center of the rink. She was holding the nutcracker as she performed the Clara routine. Jill went through every move in her mind. She knew the role by heart.

As Jill watched, she had to admit that Amber was doing very well. But she also realized that Kathy was right. The Dewdrop Fairy role was much more demanding. It really *was* a showcase for Jill's talent as a skater. Amber's solos were short, and they were a lot easier than Jill's.

Now that Jill thought about it, she realized that Clara spent most of the second act sitting on the throne while the other skaters paraded before her. In fact, Jill realized, of all the parts in the show, hers was the best for any junior skater. It was almost as difficult as Trisha McCoy's beautiful solo as the Sugarplum Fairy.

Jill couldn't have felt happier. But she also felt a little silly. She had spent so much time worrying about Amber's skating the Clara role that she hadn't noticed how good a part she had herself.

The taping continued, and Jill watched every bit of

it. Tori's mouse solo was good—and very funny. Tori seemed pleased. Her face was glowing with excitement when she took off her mouse head. Haley and Patrick also did really well.

When the taping was over, all the Silver Blades skaters met in a corner of the rink. Jill stood with Ryan, and Haley brought her dad. Patrick, Tori, and Amber pulled Kathy over. Dan lifted his camera.

"All right, everybody, big smile!" He snapped another picture.

"But Dan," Haley said, "we don't have any pictures of you!"

"I'll take it," Ryan offered. "Say cheese!"

"Don't even mention cheese," Tori groaned. "I've had it with mice for the rest of my life."

Everybody laughed, and Ryan took the photo. They all agreed to meet later for dinner. Then everyone went to change out of their costumes.

As Jill turned toward the dressing room Ludmila called out to her. Jill's heart started pounding.

"Jill," Ludmila said, "may I speak with you for a moment?"

Jill hurried toward her. "Hi, Ludmila," she said shyly.

"You were terrific," Ludmila told her. "I just had to tell you—your performance was very impressive."

"Thank you," Jill said.

"Truly exceptional," Ludmila went on. "Excellent work, Jill. And now I think you're ready to come back to the Academy. How about after the holidays? What do you think?"

Jill couldn't believe it. Ludmila acted as if there had never been any question of not asking Jill back.

"There's nothing I'd like more!" Jill was so happy that she threw her arms around the Russian coach.

Ludmila looked surprised, but gave Jill a big hug in return. "Now go tell Bronya she is getting her roommate back," Ludmila suggested.

Jill hurried across the rink. No doubt about it, she thought. Sometimes dreams really do come true.

14

Jill heard a noise and opened her eyes. For a moment she thought she was still in her hotel room in Boston. But then she saw her Katarina Witt poster hanging on her closet door, and she knew she was back home in Seneca Hills. It was Christmas Day. And it was also the day that *Nutcracker on Ice* would be shown on TV!

Jill had arrived the day before, in time to spend a quiet Christmas Eve with her family. That night there would be a party for the members of Silver Blades at Dan's house. They all planned to watch the ice show together.

Randi bounced onto Jill's bed. "Come on, Jill, get up!" Randi yanked back the covers. "It's time to open presents!"

"Let's go, then," Jill said.

A few minutes later the entire Wong family was gathered around their tree. Mrs. Wong carried in a tea tray for herself and her husband. Mr. Wong rubbed his eyes and pretended to fall back asleep. Michael and Mark jumped on his lap.

"Daddy, wake up! It's Christmas!" they yelled together.

"Santa was here!" Michael declared.

"He left presents under the tree," Mark added.

"Well, we'd better open them, don't you think?" Mr. Wong gave Jill a wink.

"I have something just for you, Jill," Kristi said. She handed Jill a tube-shaped gift.

Jill pulled off the wrapping paper and unrolled a sheet of paper. It was a drawing of stars and planets. A figure of Jill stood in the middle. Underneath, it said, "Our own star, Jill Wong."

"Thank you, Kristi! It's beautiful. I'll hang it in my room when I go back to the Academy," Jill promised. All of a sudden she felt tears coming, but she blinked them back. She was going to miss her family so much!

Kristi got a telescope and a book about stars. Henry got the bongo drums he'd asked for. Michael and Mark were already playing with their new toy dinosaurs.

"Hey, where's my present?" Randi demanded.

Suddenly there was the sound of barking from the kitchen.

"Did you hear that?" Mrs. Wong asked. "Randi, would you look in the kitchen and see what that funny noise was?"

Randi was up and running. In a minute she came back hugging a little black puppy. It had white paws and a white patch over one eye. Randi was grinning from ear to ear.

"I'm going to name him Pirate," Randi declared. "He already has an eye patch."

Everybody laughed. Then the doorbell rang.

"I'll get it," Jill said, jumping up.

It was Ryan.

"Merry Christmas. I wanted to bring you this," he said, holding out a small box with silver bows.

"But you already gave me a present," Jill said, surprised. She lifted her wrist and showed off the bracelet Ryan had given her. The gold hearts glimmered.

"That was for good luck," Ryan told her. "This is your real present. It goes with the first one."

"Well, I have something for you, too," Jill said. "Wait a second, I'll be right back."

Jill ran inside and grabbed Ryan's present from under the tree.

"You first," Jill said. She handed Ryan his gift.

Ryan ripped open the paper. "Wow! This is great!" He held up a large photograph in a fancy silver frame. It showed Ryan and Jill, right after she had skated the Dewdrop Fairy routine.

"I never want you to forget that moment," Jill said.

"Me either," Ryan agreed. Ryan handed Jill the present he'd brought.

Jill opened the small box and smiled. Inside was a gold charm in the shape of a fairy.

"I thought you could put it on the bracelet," Ryan said.

"Oh, Ryan, it's beautiful."

"I'm going to miss you," Ryan told her. He leaned forward and gave Jill a kiss.

"I'm going to miss you, too," Jill said.

~ ~

Later that day, Jill went to Dan's house for the Silver Blades Christmas party. The house was small and cozy. There was one large glass case filled with Dan's skating trophies. Everyone was gathered in the living room, drinking punch and eating cookies. Amber sat on the couch with Haley, Patrick, and Tori. Jill, Danielle, and Nikki sat on the floor on big pillows. Martina was perched in a big armchair.

Kathy arrived and quickly slipped off her dark blue parka. For once, her dark blond hair was loose.

"Wow, Kathy—no ponytail!" Haley cried.

"It's Christmas! Even *I* take the day off," Kathy replied with a laugh. "By the way, everyone, I saw Mr. Weiler earlier. He's home now, though he's still pretty weak. He asked me to wish everyone a merry Christmas and a happy new year. I gave him all your holiday cards."

"I hope he visits us at the rink soon," Tori said. Her eyes darted to the television. "Look, the show is starting! Let's turn it up!"

The skaters were quiet as the program began. The first scene showed Clara and her family getting ready for a big Christmas party. Jill glanced at Amber, who was watching the TV intently.

The party scene came next. Bronya and Marie skated under the Christmas tree, playing hide-and-seek.

"Those are my friends from the Academy," Jill said, pointing them out.

Amber's first Clara solo began. Jill thought Amber's skating was even more impressive now that she saw it on TV. There was no doubt that Amber was very talented.

"Wow, you were great, Amber!" Martina exclaimed when the solo ended.

Amber beamed. "Thanks."

"This is so exciting!" Nikki cried. "I can't wait to see the rest of you guys."

"Be sure to watch for me in the battle of the mice," Tori said. "Not that you can tell who I am in that silly mouse costume."

Tori's solo came on. She had to jump and leap as if she were being chased by a cat. Best of all, she landed her double salchow–double toe loop perfectly.

"Tori, that was great!" Nikki said, laughing. "You were so funny."

"Wasn't I?" Tori said smugly. "I thought I added something special to the scene."

"You mean you added some *ham* to the cheese," Haley teased her. Everyone laughed.

"By the way, Dan," Tori said, "I never did say thank you for getting me that solo. I really do appreciate it."

"You're a super skater," Dan said. "You did a great job."

Tori and Amber were so proud of their solos. Jill was getting excited about seeing her own solo. She hoped it was coming up soon.

Finally the second act started. Amber had her big scene with Christopher Kane. They skated well together around the set of the Land of Sweets. Then came Haley and Patrick. They looked great in their pairs routine. Jill glanced at them when it was over. They were both grinning from ear to ear.

"Jill! There you are!" Haley screamed.

Jill had seen herself on videotape many times before. But she was amazed at the effect of her beautiful costume under the professional lighting.

"Jill, you were amazing," Danielle said when her solo was over. "That's the best I've ever seen you skate!"

"I hope I skate as well as you someday," Amber added.

"Thanks, Amber, but you're already a great skater," Jill replied, returning the compliment.

The show came to an end with Christopher Kane and Trisha McCoy skating a romantic finale. Then Clara and the Nutcracker Prince sailed away in a swan sleigh, waving good-bye to everyone in the Land of Sweets. All the Silver Blades skaters burst into applause.

"That was such a great show. I'm sorry it's over." Martina sighed. "I hope I can be on TV someday."

"Wait—the interviews are next," Tori said. "I can't wait to see your family profile, Jill. I wonder if they put me in anywhere."

"We'll soon find out," Haley teased.

Jill swallowed nervously. She had almost forgotten about her interview. Would they show the part where she said all those stupid things? Jill eyed Kathy. How would she ever explain to her coach?

Suddenly the Wong family filled the TV screen. Everybody screamed with laughter when the twins wouldn't talk. There was even a shot of Henry's pet tarantula. Then came the scene of Jill practicing. Jill winced as she watched herself falling and getting back up to start all over again.

"Oh, great!" Jill exclaimed. "They *would* have to show that!"

"It's definitely part of skating," Kathy said.

Then came Jill's interview. Everyone settled down to listen.

"When I'm skating, nothing else matters," Jill said. "It makes me happier than anything else."

Jill hoped she didn't sound too corny.

Then came the part Jill had been dreading. "Kathy is a great coach for me here," she heard herself say. "And Ludmila is a great coach at the Academy."

"Well said," Kathy told Jill. "That was a tough question, and you handled it exactly right."

Jill sighed with relief.

Amber's profile was next. There were lots of shots of Amber on the ice, performing her most difficult jumps and spins. Then the scene shifted to Amber and her mom in the Seneca Hills Motel. Jill was startled. The motel room was bare. It didn't look like a very nice place to spend Christmas.

Amber's mom was saying that the Armstrongs didn't have much money to spend on Amber's skating career. She and Amber had taken a bus all the way from New Mexico to Seneca Hills. "It was just too expensive to fly," Mrs. Armstrong said. She looked sad as she explained how Amber's father had to stay behind. He couldn't afford to leave his job. Then there was a close-up of Amber. She also looked unhappy when she talked about having her family split apart.

Jill glanced at Amber as she watched the interview. Amber's shoulders were hunched, and she twisted her hands in her lap.

Amber's mom came on again. She spoke in a tired voice. "I guess all skating families have to make some sacrifices," she said. "But it's worth it to see Amber succeed. We're so proud of her."

I guess Amber doesn't have much of a family life anymore, Jill realized. And it didn't look like much fun living in the Seneca Hills Motel.

At the end of the interview, another big close-up of Amber filled the screen.

"Is there anything else that you enjoy as much as skating?" the interviewer asked. "How about friends? Having fun?"

Amber shook her head. "Skating is my whole life," she said.

Jill realized that there was a big difference between her and Amber. They had certain things in common. Both were talented skaters, and both families made sacrifices for their skating. But Jill saw that she had a lot more going for her than Amber did. She had a big, supportive family. And she had good friends. And on top of that, she was going to the Ice Academy in Denver. The last bit of anger Jill felt toward Amber melted away.

The program was over. Dan turned off the TV and popped out the videocassette he'd used to tape the show.

"We can add this to our Silver Blades collection," he said. He smiled at Kathy. "Our skaters looked great, don't you think?"

"Absolutely." Kathy raised her glass of punch. "To Silver Blades!"

Everyone joined in the toast.

"To Jill," Martina added. "We'll miss you, but I hope you have a great year back at the Academy."

Everyone toasted again.

"Your performance really was amazing," Nikki added. "No wonder they asked you back."

"Thanks, everybody." Jill started to blush a little. "I'm going to miss you guys. But I'm also glad they want me to return."

"I'm really happy for you, Jill," Amber said.

Jill smiled. "Thanks, Amber."

Everyone broke into small groups and kept talking. Amber leaned closer to Jill.

"I guess you leave for the Academy pretty soon," Amber said. "It sounds great. You know, I was invited to a school, too. But it was in Paris. I couldn't really go so far away."

So I was right, Jill thought. Amber *was* the other skater. Jill had called the European scouts even before they got back to her with a decision. She had told them that she was flattered by their interest but that she would be returning to the Ice Academy. She would never know to whom the European scouts had planned to offer the open slot first—her or Amber—but it didn't matter anymore.

"Besides, I already love it here at Silver Blades," Amber was saying.

"You'll do great in Seneca Hills," Jill said, and she meant it. "Amber," she added slowly, "do you remember talking to Ludmila the day before the taping? I think she asked you something."

Amber frowned, trying to remember. "Oh, yeah. She asked if I had seen her sweater anywhere. She thought she had left it at the rink," she answered. "Why?"

Jill burst out laughing. "Just curious."

"What's so funny?" Tori demanded, plopping down next to Jill.

Jill shook her head. "Me! I've been making a big deal out of nothing! And boy, was I wrong about things." Like thinking Ludmila wanted Amber to go to the Academy. And thinking that the Dewdrop Fairy wasn't a good role. And thinking that Amber was trying to take everything away from me. I should be careful about that in the future, Jill decided.

"Hey," Jill told Tori, "I just thought of my New Year's resolution."

"What?" Tori asked.

"No more jumping to conclusions." Jill laughed. "From now on, I'll save my jumps for the ice."

#5: The Perfect Pair

Nikki Simon and Alex Beekman are the perfect pair on the ice. But off the ice there's a big problem. Suddenly Alex is sending Nikki gifts and asking her out on dates. Nikki wants to be Alex's partner in pairs but not his girlfriend. Will she lose Alex when she tells him? Can Nikki's friends in Silver Blades find a way to save her friendship with Alex *and* her skating career?

#6: Skating Camp

Summer's here and Jill Wong can't wait to join her best friends from Silver Blades at skating camp. It's going to be just like old times. But things have changed since Jill left Silver Blades to train at a famous ice academy. Tori and Danielle are spending all their time with another skater, Haley Arthur, and Nikki has a big secret that she won't share with anyone. Has Jill lost her best friends forever?

#7: The Ice Princess

Tori's favorite skating superstar, Elyse Taylor, is in town, and she's staying with Tori! When Elyse promises to teach Tori her famous spin, Tori's sure they'll become the best of friends. But Elyse isn't the sweet champion everyone thinks she is. And she's out to get Tori in *big* trouble!

#8: Rumors at the Rink

Haley can't believe it—Kathy Bart, her favorite coach in the whole world, is quitting Silver Blades! Haley's sure it's all her fault. Why didn't she listen when everyone told her to stop playing practical jokes on Kathy?

With Kathy gone, Haley knows she'll never win the next big competition. She has to make Kathy change her mind—no matter what. But will Haley's secret plan work?

#9: Spring Break

Jill is home from the Ice Academy, and everyone is treating her like a star. And she loves it! It's like a dream come true—especially when she meets cute, fifteen-year-old Ryan McKensey. He's so fun and cool—and he happens to be her number-one fan!

The only problem is that he doesn't understand what it takes to be a professional athlete. Jill doesn't want to ruin her chances with such a great guy. But will dating Ryan destroy her future as an Olympic skater?

#10: Center Ice

It's gold medal time for Tori—she just knows it! The next big competition is coming up, and Tori has a winning routine. Now all she needs is that fabulous skating dress her mother promised her. But Mrs. Carsen doesn't seem to be interested in Tori's skating anymore—not since she started dating a new man in town. When Mrs. Carsen tells Tori she's not going to the competition, Tori decides enough is enough. She has a plan that will change everything—forever!

#11: A Surprise Twist

Danielle's on top of the world! All her hard work at the rink has paid off. She's good. Very good. And Dani's new English teacher, Ms. Howard, says she has a real flair for writing—she might even be the best writer in her class. Trouble is, there's a big skating competition coming up—*and* a writing contest. Dani's stumped. Her friends and family are counting on her to skate her best. But Ms. Howard is counting on her to write a winning story. How can Dani choose between skating and her new passion?

#12: The Winning Spirit

A group of Special Olympics skaters is on the way to Seneca Hills! The skaters are going to pair up with the Silver Blades members in a minicompetition. Everyone in Silver Blades thinks Nikki Simon is really lucky—her Special Olympics partner is Carrie, a girl with Down syndrome who's one of the best visiting skaters. But Nikki can't seem to warm up to the idea of skating with Carrie. In fact, she seems to be hiding something . . . but what?

#13: The Big Audition

Holiday excitement is in the air! Jill Wong, one of Silver Blades' best skaters, is certain she will win the leading role of Clara in the *Nutcracker on Ice* spectacular—until young skater Amber Armstrong comes along. At first Jill can't believe that Amber is serious competition. But she had better believe it—and fast! Because she's about to find herself completely out of the spotlight.